JR

CELG

D0885917

SPECIAL MESSAGE TO READERS

THE ULVERSCROFT FOUNDATION
(registered UK charity number 264873)
was established in 1972 to provide funds for
research, diagnosis and treatment of eye diseases.
Examples of major projects funded by
the Ulverscroft Foundation are:-

- The Children's Eye Unit at Moorfields Eye
  Hospital, London
- The Ulverscroft Children's Eye Unit at Great
  Ormond Street Hospital for Sick Children
- Funding research into eye diseases and
  treatment at the Department of Ophthalmology,
  University of Leicester
- The Ulverscroft Vision Research Group,
  Institute of Child Health
- Twin operating theatres at the Western
  Ophthalmic Hospital, London
- The Chair of Ophthalmology at the Royal
  Australian College of Ophthalmologists

You can help further the work of the Foundation
by making a donation or leaving a legacy.
Every contribution is gratefully received. If you
would like to help support the Foundation or
require further information, please contact:

THE ULVERSCROFT FOUNDATION
The Green, Bradgate Road, Anstey
Leicester LE7 7FU, England
Tel: (0116) 236 4325

website: www.foundation.ulverscroft.com

DIABLO

On the streets of Diablo jobs are scarce, tempers roil, and dead men are stripped almost before they hit the ground. But Shawn Brodie needs to collect $3,000 for Tin Can Evans, and that amount of money can cause epic problems for a man in a hell of a town such as this. With a host of dangerous men walking its streets, it's only a matter of time before the fuse is lit that threatens to blow Diablo all to Hell . . . which may be where it belongs.

Books by Chuck Tyrell
in the Linford Western Library:

VULTURE GOLD
GUNS OF PONDEROSA
THE KILLING TRAIL
HELL FIRE IN PARADISE
A MAN CALLED BREED
DOLLAR A DAY
ROAD TO RIMROCK
MONTY McCORD

CHUCK TYRELL

◆

DIABLO

Complete and Unabridged

LINFORD
Leicester

First published in Great Britain in 2014 by
Robert Hale Limited
London

First Linford Edition
published 2016
by arrangement with
Robert Hale Limited
London

Copyright © 2014 by Chuck Tyrell
All rights reserved

A catalogue record for this book is available
from the British Library.

ISBN 978–1–4448–2755–2

Published by
F. A. Thorpe (Publishing)
Anstey, Leicestershire

Set by Words & Graphics Ltd.
Anstey, Leicestershire
Printed and bound in Great Britain by
T. J. International Ltd., Padstow, Cornwall

This book is printed on acid-free paper

when he got tossed into Yuma's hell hole at fourteen. He learned a lot in the pen, and he'd learned a lot since. 'Maybe he thinks he's tough enough that he don't need to pay what he owes.'

'I'll talk a little sense into him,' Shawn said.

'May take more'n a little, boy.'

Shawn held his hand out. 'Out front,' he said.

Tin Can grinned. 'That's my boy. Always businesslike.'

'You taught me, old man.'

'Done a good job of it, too.' Tin Can waved at one of his bearers, a big man of placid nature. 'Coffee for Mr Brodie and me,' he said.

'Yessir, Mr Evans,' the man said and left the room.

'Let me see your hands,' Tin Can said. He held his own out, palms up.

Shawn laid his right hand on Tin Can's palm.

Tin Can looked closely, clucking his tongue at the scars and fingering the

3

knotted calluses on the first and second knuckles. 'Can you still break two-bys?'

'If it comes to that.'

'Never could see the smarts of dancing around, kicking the air and stuff,' Tin Can said.

'Do it every day and your body learns all the moves and they come natural when there's a need.'

The big man came back in with two stoneware mugs. He put one in front of Tin Can and gave the other to Shawn. Tin Can took a sip. Shawn let his sit.

'Not into coffee these days?' Tin Can said.

'Let'n it cool. Hot stuff in a man's mouth can throw his coordination off.'

'You always so careful?'

Shawn smiled. 'Whenever a man's in the same room with Tin Can Evans, 'twould pay him well to be extra careful,' he said.

Tin Can rolled his wheeled chair around and back to the Miller safe in the corner. He twiddled the dial, keeping his body between the safe and Shawn.

'I ain't interested in the combination to your goldurn safe,' Shawn said.

'Can't afford any mistakes, Shawn. If I play loose with you, I'll likely do so with someone who's looking to steal all I've got . . . which ain't all that much.'

Shawn barked a laugh. 'That's a pile of buffalo chips if ever I heard one.'

Tin Can held out a sheaf of bills. 'I'm fronting you three hundred for this one, Shawn. And I've got no idea how to go about collecting that debt.'

Shawn noticed the tremble in Tin Can's hand as he passed over the bills. 'I'll do what I can, Tin Can. If I can't get your money, I'll give this back.' He flourished the handful of greenbacks, then paused a moment. 'What's up, Tin Can? Ain't like you to be so nervous.'

Tin Can clammed up. His mouth became a thin strip across his face. His brow furrowed. Then he laughed heartily, but Shawn could tell it was a forced laugh.

'Me? Nah. Old age, maybe. But anyway. Whenever a man starts using money to make money, the worries multiply. Ain't everyone's a good borrower. Fact is, a man's all humble and as-you-please when he borrows, making promises and such, but as soon as he stops hurting, it gets harder and harder to see himself as someone who was down and out and borrowed money to tide himself over. Then the interest he agreed upon becomes a millstone, some kind of unfairly heavy weight hanging around his neck. Shee-it. I'm not complaining. Only so many things a man in my shoes can do, 'cept I ain't got no shoes.'

It was the longest speech Shawn had ever heard from Tin Can Evans. 'If you're worried, Tin Can, you know you can count on me.'

'Yeah, I know, kid. I'll keep that in mind. And you can check the Western Union offices now and again, see if there's a message from me. You know how it goes.'

'Yeah, I know.' Shawn tucked the bills into his pocket. Wells Fargo'd be the first stop. Three years out of Yuma. Three years of collecting for Tin Can Evans. Three years of ignoring his mother and Fen Dillard at Grant's Crossing. Even though he sent money to Madam Moustache in Tombstone for his little sister Abby's room and board, he still stood more than $1,000 to the good, and today's front money would add $150 to that. 'Reckon I'll trot on down to Diablo and check out the lay of the land.'

'One more thing,' Tin Can said. 'I hear rumors of Chinaman trouble over to Diablo. Don't you go getting mixed up in that and come back here to Winslow in a pine box, you hear?'

'I got no interest in Chinamen.'

'Good. Keep it that way, that's all.'

After a moment Shawn put on his Stetson and stepped out of Tin Can's house.

★   ★   ★

Canyon Diablo goes in a straight line across the Great Colorado Plateau to the Little Colorado River, but it twists and turns along that line like a rattler heading for a rat's hole. Amiel Whipple noted its hellish nature and named the place when he surveyed a railroad route south of the Grand Canyon in '53. But for some reason, the deep pockets that financed the Atlantic & Pacific hadn't figured on a full-sized trestle across Canyon Diablo. So the rails stopped at the east bank.

Men and material piled up at the edge. Some meant for the railway, some to be trans-shipped by wagon to Flagstaff, Prescott, and points west. A store went up. Tarpaper shacks dotted the low hills. The Chinese lived in the swale between the meteor crater and the canyon rim, keeping to the south side of the tracks. If a man wanted to sleep it off in an opium den, he went over to Chinkburg, as the whites called the place. For forty-rod rotgut, though, stuff cobbled together of grain alcohol, plug tobacco, Tabasco sauce, and rattlesnake heads, a man need only step into one of the fourteen saloons that lined the main drag, appropriately called Hell Street.

A train came once a day. Sometimes people got off. Sometimes they got on. Iron rails rode the flat cars, supplies for towns further west rode the freight cars, and sometimes horses and cows rode in the cattle cars. Laborers lined up for a chance to unload the cars. This flow of supplies and people provided employment for townspeople and was reason enough to stage a hold-up.

The Irishmen inhabited the north side of Diablo, and they acted as if they owned the whole town. A&P built a siding on each side of the main track, and fancy passenger cars sat on those sidings, housing railroad men and others who could pay the railroad for their use.

Ma Greeson put up a canvas-and-slab boarding house where men slept as many as a dozen to the room. Five of the fourteen saloons on Hell Street had second stories where a man could spend the night if he paid the price. And, considering the warmth and companionship, sometimes it seemed cheap enough. Especially after a few rounds of what passed for whiskey.

Once the Mississippi had been the lifeline for Samuel Jones, and before that he lived a life of ease in New Orleans. He hit what he aimed at with a pistol, Derringer or Remington. When he got off the A&P cars at Diablo, he had Maisie Worthington on his arm, three packs of playing cards in his pocket, and a long ivory-tipped cane in his hand. Together they ambled east on Hell Street, looking for Keno Harry's Poker Flat.

Jones ignored the covetous glances and avaricious stares elicited by his pearl-gray frock-coat and striped California pants, the obviously expensive gold watch chain across his silk vest and the diamond-looking stickpin in his cravat. His dress was dated, pre-war, in fact. So it set him apart from the rabble and that was important when making an entrance to a new fold where new sheep waited to be fleeced. He knew Diablo by reputation. Diablo, the town with no law. Diablo, a patch of Hell, as its name implied.

Nor was Maisie unprepared for the hellhole called Diablo. Her parasol and flouncy dress said Southern belle, as did her mincing step. Such was her figure that few men noticed the hardness in her ice-blue eyes or the determined set of her jaw. The dusky tone of her skin indicated to those knowledgeable about such things that she was probably octoroon or some such. Men licked their lips when Maisie Worthington passed, and their eyes were hot as they watched her walk.

From the stone station house Sam and Maisie paraded down Hell Street. Across from the station stood Hall's Wagon & Warehouse. Goods bound for Flagstaff and Prescott, Green Valley and Pleasant Valley, Kingman and Jerome, and points south and west often sat in Hall's warehouse until freight wagons could haul them to their destinations.

Further along the street stood Bartlett's Merchantile, Colorado saloon, Bughouse Joe's, Annie's House of Joy. Sounds of a fiddler and stomping feet came from the Cootchy Clatch dance hall even though the sun was high and hot and most of Diablo's denizens were thinking of a noon meal, or lack of one, or a drink for breakfast, anything but dancing.

Poker Flat stood between the Texas Saloon and B S Mary's, a house of ill repute. 'Ah, our destination,' Sam said, just loud enough for Maisie to hear.

She giggled and clutched his arm closer. 'Two slimy-looking gents is following us'ns, Samuel,' she said. 'Should we run away? Or should we let them have their say?'

'I noticed them, my dear. Let's let events progress in a natural manner, I'd say. Have your little friend ready, please.'

Maisie laughed, the high tinkling of a

To Deon and Darv,
the best brothers
a man could ever wish for

conquest of the South Side.

Before Tin Can got out of Yuma, Shawn had collected $2,000 from Fen Dillard, the man who married his ma. That earned him $200 to start and another $200 when he turned the cash over to Tin Can.

'Who's Ellison Peel?' Shawn asked.

'A slimy son of a bitch,' Tin Can said.

'Slimier'n you?' Shawn held his face expressionless, though he spoke in jest. He'd found Tin Can honest in his own way, and always concerned about fair play.

'Somewhat,' Tin Can said. 'Somewhat. He's crooked as a dog's hind leg, but would have people think otherwise. Most of the time, anyway.'

'How come he don't pay what's due?'

'He's begged off for more'n a year now, and I figure my money's made enough for him already. Diablo ain't got no law, son. And Peel's got quite a gang protecting him.' Tin Can paused, taking gauge of Shawn's face. He wasn't the whiskerless kid he'd been

1

'This one ain't gonna be no pushover, boy,' Tin Can Evans said. 'I need you to collect three thousand from Ellison Peel over to Diablo.'

Shawn Brodie shrugged. 'None of your jobs are pushovers, Tin Can. So far, I've figured out a way.'

Tin Can laughed, a loud braying sound that belied the fact that he was a small man with legs that only extended to mid-thigh. After serving his time in Yuma territorial prison, Tin Can moved his headquarters to Winslow, a major stop on the Atlantic & Pacific Railroad. But now the rail-laying had stopped at the edge of Canyon Diablo, and Winslow's growth slowed.

With some of the money he'd made in prison, Tin Can Evans bought the Silver Dollar saloon on the wrong side of the tracks in Winslow, and started his

1

no-brain Southern woman. 'Oh my, sir. You flatter me,' she said, loud enough for the men behind them to hear. She reached into her drawstring bag and cocked the double-barreled .41 Derringer that habitually resided there.

'Get 'um!' Two would-be robbers rushed at Sam and Maisie from behind. The fact that they didn't shoot first and rob later said they were on the lower end of Diablo's ne'er-do-well population. They brandished heavy sticks and rushed to club Sam and Maisie to the dust of Hell Street.

'Gentlemen, gentlemen,' Sam said as he flicked his cane and drew a slim blade from it. The steel came free and whipped up to catch the first robber in the throat, just below the larynx. He fell, choking, clutching his torn throat, trying to speak, eyes wide with fear.

Maisie's Derringer barked, then barked again. Robber number two folded and dropped to the rocky road. He trembled a moment, kicked twice, then went limp.

'Well done, my dear,' Sam said.

The man he'd skewered scrambled to his feet and staggered away, his hands still clutching his bleeding throat.

'Are you letting him go?' Maisie asked.

'No doctors in Diablo,' Sam said. 'None I've heard of, anyway. Let him be an object lesson. Once we've fleeced the sheep, we'll move on.'

'Indeed,' Maisie said.

'Reload your little friend, my dear. This is not New Orleans.' Sam Jones reinserted the fine steel blade of his sword into the sheath that formed his cane. His own Derringer lay in a clip on his arm.

'Sam! Samuel Jones! I'll swear. A sight for sore eyes, ye are.' Keno Harry looked both ways before he crossed Hell Street.

'Good to see you, Harry. Wolf Creek wasn't the same without you.' Sam met Keno Harry's outstretched hand with his own.

Men had already gathered around

them. Their eyes were not so much on the three gamblers as watching the body at their feet.

'Come on, come on. Poker Flat awaits. Sheep for the taking.' Harry led Sam and Maisie across the street and into his gambling parlor. Just before entering, Sam glanced back at the body of the would-be robber. Little fistfights broke out over his boots, which were in surprisingly good condition. The body already lay naked in the street.

Harry noticed Sam's look. 'Not to worry. They'll plant him outside of town somewhere after they've checked his teeth. Could be some gold in them, you know. Come on. I've got some good whiskey to cut the smoke you had to eat on that train.'

'A small shot of Jameson would do well,' Sam said. 'Don't you think so, my dear?'

'Bourbon. Rye. Irish. Any old whiskey will do. As long as it's whiskey and not some warlock's brew of grain alcohol and snake heads,' Maisie said. 'I don't take to cold tea, either, though I've drunk my share of that awful stuff.'

Harry chuckled. 'I wouldn't want to get on your wrong side, young lady. I saw what you did with that little Derringer.'

'A woman's got the right to protect herself when there's no willing gentleman at hand to do the job for her.'

Harry waved them to seats at the single empty table, and signaled to the barkeep, raising two fingers and thumping his own chest.

The barkeep brought a bottle of Old Potrero and three glasses. Harry poured; two fingers for Sam and Maisie, and three for himself. 'Here's to fleeced sheep,' he said, lifting the glass.

'Fleece is a favorite of mine,' Sam Jones said, 'and Maisie here is particularly good in the fleecing business.' He took a healthy swig but didn't knock the whiskey back. Maisie sipped at hers, then sighed.

'You. Son. Of. A. Bitch!'

The shout came from a poker game three tables away. A heavy man sitting on a high chair near the bar snapped his 10-gauge Parker closed and eared the hammers back. His voice had a hard edge to it, and everyone in the joint heard every word.

'Keep your hands on the table, all of you. I don't want to kill no one who don't deserve it, but I'll kill ya all if you're not civil to each other.' He stepped off the high chair and ambled over to the table.

'What's sticking in your craw, young-ster?' he asked the man who'd shouted.

'Sumbitch's second dealing. I seen 'im.'

The shotgun enforcer looked hard at the shark. 'This man got good eyes?'

The gambler started to say something, then clamped his mouth shut.

'How much you lose?' the enforcer asked the youngster.

'Near on to a hunnert.'

'You are aware that poker is a game of chance. Right?'

The youngster gulped. 'Yeah,' he finally said.

'OK, shark. I'm giving you the benefit of the doubt. Give the man fifty dollars, and you can stay. But at Poker Flat, no one takes an unfair edge. That clear?'

'Of course,' the gambler said. He plucked some eagles from the pile of coins in front of him and pushed them across the table. 'Sorry about the misunderstanding. Won't you sit down and continue the game?'

The youngster pulled the gold coins on across the table, picked them up, and shoved them in a pocket.

Harry stood and walked over to the table. 'What's your name, son?'

'Billy. Billy Daggs.'

'Your pa know you're gambling in Diablo?'

'Uh-uh.'

'Jim. Dallas. Come on over here.'

Two more enforcers came from the corners of the room.

'Gentlemen, you are to escort Billy

Daggs to the Daggs place north of Flagstaff. Don't want news of him getting robbed on the way, either. Clear?'

'Yeah, boss,' the gunmen chorused. They escorted young Billy Daggs out the door of Poker Flat with Peacemakers drawn.

'Nicely done, Harry,' Sam said.

'I'll keep an eye on that sharp. He cheats in my house and he'll not live to cheat anywhere else.'

'Good you have plenty of backup.'

'Any other town and you'd turn it over to the marshal. In Diablo, you bury your own dead and find your own ways to stay alive. Here there ain't no law but the ones you make for yourself.'

'I think I like this town already,' Maisie said. 'Honey, can we stay awhile?'

2

Shawn Brodie rode twenty miles north of Diablo, almost to the Little Colorado River. While Canyon Diablo ran water only when rains passed over, the Little Colorado started in the rancherias of the White Mountain Apaches and, fed by the Zuni and Puerco Rivers and Clear Creek, it ran its way north and west across the Great Colorado Plateau. The Little Colorado always ran water. And Ellison Peel had a ranch that used Little Colorado water. For a man who'd been down and almost out three years ago, Peel'd come a long way.

Cottonwoods and willows lined the river, but they grew only in the bottoms of Canyon Diablo. Cows ate the short grass on the plateau, then worked their way down into the canyon bottoms for the sweet grass that grew there. It was hell getting them out again.

Shawn rode General, the horse he got from Warden Justin Strickland when he was pardoned out of Yuma. A man would have to go a long way to find a better horse than General. He paid no attention to the jackrabbit that leaped almost from under his hoofs and bounded across the arid land. General was not a horse easily spooked.

A column of dust rose from a flat some distance to the northwest. Likely men working animals. Shawn gigged General in that direction. Before he could see the source of the dust, he heard lowing cattle, mama cows calling for babies. That meant a branding. Shawn grinned.

Quarter of an hour later he topped a low rise that let him see the cause of the dust. Four cowboys held maybe fifty cows in a makeshift corral with the calves outside. A fire burned off to the south and branding-irons stuck out of the coals like spokes on an old wagon wheel. Two riders head-and-heeled calves while a third applied brands and a fourth cut earmarks and castrated the baby bulls. It wasn't easy work, and the cowboys sweated.

General stood quietly near the east side of the corral for several minutes before anyone noticed him and his rider.

'Looking for grub, we ain't got none,' the man with the knife hollered.

'Need any help?' Shawn hollered back.

'Ain't hiring,' came the answer.

Shawn dismounted and left General ground tied. He walked over to the fire, gathered the branding-irons that had been used and then tossed in the general direction of the fire in hopes they'd somehow go back in proper. Shawn arranged them properly, taking care not to knock over the coffee pot.

The brander plucked a hot iron from the fire. 'Obliged,' he barely had time to say before the next calf was stretched out and helpless, ready to be indelibly marked for life.

Shawn kept the irons hot until all the

calves were branded, earmarked, and castrated. The cowboy with the Barlow knife dabbed the calves' wounds with pine tar oil to keep the blowflies off until they scabbed over.

The man who seemed to boss the cowboys opened the gate of the corral and let the momma cows rush out to find and comfort their calves. The cowboys got tin cups from their war bags and gathered round the branding-fire for coffee. Shawn pulled the irons from the fire and put them aside to cool. The brand was Lazy EP: Ellison Peel's mark. Exactly what Shawn was hoping to find.

'You got a cup?' the cowboy brander asked.

Shawn shook his head. 'Ain't got nothing much,' he said.

'I'm Guy Rankin,' the cowboy said.

'Shawn Brodie.'

'Riding grubline?'

'Looking for work,' Shawn said. 'Thought of drifting over toward Flagstaff. Hashknife ain't hiring.'

'Ain't many outfits hiring,' Rankin said. 'You don't wear a gun, neither.'

Shawn grinned. 'Guns get people killed,' he said. 'Not many'll shoot a down-and-out rannie who's not packing. I'm partial to staying alive.'

'Smart or dumb, don't know which.'

'Dumb, I'd say,' a cowboy said. ''Specially if you're going anywhere near Diablo.'

'Heard it's a tough town,' Shawn said.

'Tough ain't the right word. They named the main drag Hell Street. Good place to die.'

'I been in Hell,' Shawn said. 'Yuma.'

'No shit?'

Shawn nodded.

Rankin held out his cup. 'Here, use this.'

'Obliged,' Shawn said. He took the cup and filled it half up from the pot.

'Good-looking nag ya got,' one of the riders said.

'Shawn Brodie,' Shawn said. 'Didn't get your name.'

'Nelson. Brick Nelson.'

'General over there's about as good as they get in quarter horses, I reckon.' Shawn sipped at his coffee.

'Good thing you ain't headed for Diablo, then,' Nelson said. 'Your good horse wouldn't last the night. Someone'd steal your boots ... ' Nelson's eyes strayed to see what kind of boots Shawn had on. 'Hey, you don't wear boots!' It sounded almost like an accusation.

Shawn grinned again and looked down at his moccasined feet to hide the hardness in his eyes. 'Yeah. Sometimes a man's gotta be light on his feet. Learned that in Yuma.'

'No shit. Boots keep a man's feet from getting cut up,' Rankin said. 'Don't reckon you do cowboying with them redskin shoes on.'

'Don't need boots for most things if you keep your feet hard. You wear boots when you was a kid?'

'Nah.' Rankin scratched his head. 'Never had boots until I started trailing herds on the Goodnight-Loving Trail. *Segundo* bought me a pair in Abilene as we was leaving.'

'And he ain't took 'em off since.' One of the ropers doffed his hat and ran fingers through a head of ginger hair.

Rankin puffed up at the redheaded cowboy's jibe. 'Shutchur mouth, Red. Just cause you ain't never trailed a herd.'

'I've never been on a trail drive, either,' Shawn said, as much to keep the conversation going as to take the heat off Red. 'I'm Shawn Brodie, as I said, from Grant's Crossing, and there's no drives starting from there.'

'Elliot Hart,' the red-headed cowboy said, 'but most folks just call me Red.'

'Lazy EP gonna round up soon? I sure could use a job. They say the Daggses're hiring, but I'm not all that het up on handling sheep.'

'We ain't hiring,' Rankin said. 'Least-wise so far as I know, we ain't.' He dug at the dirt with a boot toe, thinking. Then he said, 'I reckon it won't hurt nothing if you ride over to the outfit with us. Diablo's the only place close where a man can get a drink and maybe a poke, so we come up missing hands regular like.'

'Obliged,' Shawn said. He gulped the last of the coffee from the cup and handed it back to Rankin, handle first. 'Good coffee. Thanks.'

Rankin accepted the cup. 'We're done here. Reckon we'll be riding for the outfit. Coming?'

'Be right down my alley. Be good to ride with men who know what they're doing. You rannies got working cows down pat.'

'Gitchur cayuse. Let's go,' Rankin said.

The other cowboys dumped the remaining coffee on the fire, drowning most of the coals. They stomped what was left until the coals were nothing but gray powder.

Rankin mounted his sock-footed bay. 'Time to make for the Lazy EP. Let's do it.'

He led off and the others followed. Shawn brought up the rear, a smile on his lips. He'd made the first step in his plan to collect Tin Can's money from Ellison Peel.

★　★　★

Samuel Jones and Maisie Worthington's two steamer trunks arrived at Poker Flat under guard. Two men came through the door, sawed-off Greeners on their arms. They were followed by four Chinamen, two for each trunk. They made the trunks seem awfully heavy, barely managing to keep them from dragging along the floor. Two more men, armed like the other shotgunners, brought up the rear.

'Where do we put these trunks?' a shotgun man asked no one in particular.

'Butch,' Keno Harry called from a doorway at the back of the gambling house. 'Bring the trunks in here.'

The shotgunners positioned themselves where they could cover the entire
gambling room. The man called Butch
hollered at the Chinamen. 'Shoo Lee.
You Chinks haul them trunks into the
back room.'

'Yes sir, Mr Butch.' The four
Chinamen did as Butch ordered. The
shotgunners followed them.

'Against the wall,' Keno Harry said,
'one on top of the other.'

The Chinese complied, then three of
them left the room.

The shotgunners stood in a line,
hammers of their Greeners now
uncocked. The Chinese called Shoo
Lee stood to one side.

'How much?' Sam Jones asked.

'Dollar a man for the protection,'
Butch said.

'Dollar a trunk for the carry,' Shoo
Lee said.

'Shut up, Chinaman. You'll get what I
decide,' Butch growled.

Shoo Lee didn't flinch and his eyes
never left Butch's face. 'You promised

29

one dollar for each trunk,' he said, his tones icy and his face in flat hard planes. He stood relaxed yet ready, his feet shoulder width apart and his arms hanging naturally at his sides. Somehow he gave the impression of being coiled tight as a watch spring.

Sam Jones sipped from his whiskey glass. 'How much did you say you'd pay the coolies, Butch?' he asked in a flat tone.

'Umm. Well . . . '

'Butch. Out with it.' Sam's voice took on a trigger-tight quality.

'Umm. Mighta been a dollar a trunk,' Butch said.

'Might have been? Is your memory so short?'

'Dollar a trunk, that's what I said.'

Shoo Lee nodded. 'Yes,' he said. 'Dollar a trunk.'

'You were going to cheat Mr Lee and his fellows, then?' Sam asked.

'Not so much that as maybe taking a commission,' Butch said. 'Like, without us shotgunners, the Chinks wouldn't have no job at all. More'n fair, I'd say, them being pigtailed savages and all.'

Sam looked at Shoo Lee. He had no pigtail, and he still looked like a coiled spring. 'I have a feeling, Butch. If you fail to keep your word to Mr Lee, he may well take everything you have, including that fancy Greener.'

'Shee-it. One white man's worth a dozen Chinee in any kind of a scrap.'

Sam smiled. 'Really?' He shot a glance at Keno Harry. 'I've got an idea, Harry. Tell me what you think. Butch looks like a good man in a fight, maybe one of the best.'

'He's alive, and that says quite a bit in Diablo!'

'I ain't never been bested in a bare-knuckle fight,' Butch said. He unconsciously made fists and tensed his muscles.

'I'm sure that's true, Butch. I'll tell you what. I'll put up one hundred dollars. You can have it all if you can beat this pigtail-less Chinaman in a barehanded fight.'

Butch laughed. 'A hunnert dollars? That Chinaman can kiss his ass goodbye.'

'What do you think, Harry? Shall we set the fight for a week from now? Winner take all? No holds barred?'

'What does this mean? No holds barred?'

'It means you can fight any way you please.'

'Good,' Shoo Lee said. 'Seven days from right now.' He turned to Butch. 'You will lose, white man.' He gave Sam a little bow. 'One hundred dollars you promise. Say again.'

Sam said, 'In seven days, Butch . . . ' He looked at Keno Harry. 'Butch . . . ?'

'Butch Kennedy, he is,' Keno Harry said.

'Butch Kennedy will meet Shoo Lee in unarmed combat. The two shall fight for one hundred dollars in prize money. Winner take all. The winner shall be declared when either man can no longer fight. Is that satisfactory, Butch?'

The shotgunner grinned. 'Fer a

hunnert, I'd fight a grizzly.'

'Shoo Lee?'

The Oriental's eyes seemed to gleam. 'I shall be ready,' he said. 'And I will make sure you keep your promise.'

Sam gave Shoo Lee a searching look. 'Harry,' he said, 'I assume Poker Flat will take all wagers on this fight. I would like to place the equivalent of the prize money, one hundred dollars in US currency, on Shoo Lee to win. Whatever the odds.'

'Done,' Harry said.

'Butch, I'm handing Shoo Lee two dollars for hauling the trunks over here. If you want part of it, win the fight.'

Sam stepped over in front of Shoo Lee. He held out two dollars. Shoo Lee took them and bowed deeply. He bowed again, then slipped from the door into the main room. He signaled the waiting Chinese as he went, so they all left Poker Flat together.

'Well, Samuel Jones. I reckon you just set Diablo afire,' Keno Harry said.

'Well, Keno Harry, Poker Flat'll be

33

holding the wager money, right? And keep the odds, too. And do the talking that will raise interest in the fight. Should bring in a fair take, I'd say.' Sam Jones sat back down in the comfortable chair he'd occupied before getting up to pay Shoo Lee.

'My goodness, Mr Harry, would it be seemly for a little ol' girl from Nwalins to place a bet on the upcoming fisticuffs?' Maisie asked.

Harry grinned and rubbed his hands together. 'Any New Orleans belle is welcome to wager, Miss Maisie. How much and on whom?'

'What do you think, Samuel?'

'Maisie my dear, you heard me make my bet. Whether you do the same is entirely up to you.'

Maisie flounced, straightened her skirt, pulled on her sleeves, opened her drawstring bag, fished around inside it and pulled out a well-used fifty dollar bill. 'Fifty dollars, Harry,' she said.

'On which fighter?'

'Why on the winner, of course.'

Harry chuckled. 'Don't futz around with me, Miss Maisie. Just pick your winner.'

Maisie heaved a dramatic sigh. 'If you say so. I believe I'll wager my money on Shoo Lee, the Chinaman. He's got a nice tight bum, and that does not come from sitting around a gaming table. That man's got a lot more than he's letting everybody see. Yes. Fifty dollars on Shoo Lee.' She held out her hand, the crumpled bill in her palm. 'My bet,' she said.

Harry took the bill. 'I'll give you two-to-one odds, Miss Maisie. If the Chinaman wins, you'll double your money.'

News of the coming fight between Butch Kennedy and the Chinaman Shoo Lee spread through Diablo like pestilence. Men lined up to place their bets at Poker Flat. Some bet a dollar. Some bet a hundred. Some bet all they had. And Keno Harry was not a man to turn a wager away.

Butch Kennedy garnered many a free

drink as he boasted of tough men he'd met and fights he'd won.

'I remember when I was a stripling kid in Independence,' he said. He leaned against the bar while the rest of the house gambled at Poker Flat. He drained the whiskey from the glass at his elbow. 'Some fight that was.' He let out a long burp.

'Who'd ya fight, Butch? Have a drink.'

Kennedy peered at the whiskey glass in his hand. Turned it upside down, and not a single drop formed on its rim. 'Cain't drink,' he said. 'No whiskey.'

A hand held out a whiskey bottle. Kennedy fumbled with his glass. Another hand took the glass and poured whiskey into it, a good three fingers of amber. Kennedy took the whiskey with both hands and lifted it to his pursed lips.

'Who'dja fight in Independence, Butch?'

'Independence? Yeah, Independence.

Wagon trains fer Santa Fe. They loaded up in Independence.' Kennedy wiped his hand across his mouth.

'Who'd you fight, Butch?'

Kennedy gulped at the whiskey. ''Tweren't me,' he blurted. ''Twere Hank Brockman. Me, I were just a button, hardly waist high to a grown man. Brockman were the wagon master, an' he took no guff from no man. I watched him take a big ol' mule-skinner down a couple a pegs. Let me tell you, Hank Brockman could fight, no two ways about it.'

The men standing three deep around Kennedy didn't want to hear about a man named Hank Brockman whom they didn't know. They wanted Kennedy to tell of his own prowess so they'd feel safe in betting on him to beat Shoo Lee.

Kennedy finished the whiskey in his glass. 'Well then, d'I ever tell you about the time I floored Dick Evans?' He peered around at the circle of faces. Faces with bright greedy eyes. Faces with day-old and week-old and month-old beards. Faces full of avarice, wanting a champion to make money on.

'Well, me'n ol' Dick Evans squared off in the Long Branch in Dodge City, and . . . an . . . ' Kennedy's legs folded as he passed out and crumpled to the floor.

3

The white men, mostly Irish with a smattering of Italians, called the jumble of tents and shacks south of the A&P tracks Little Chinkburg. Little Chinkburg it was, but its population consisted of Chinese and blacks, Indians and Mexicans, and one Oriental from the Ryukyu Islands. When Shoo Lee left his home island of Okinawa, it was the capital of the Ryukyu Kingdom, called Loochoo by the Chinese. To maintain a modicum of independence, the kingdom paid tribute to the Chinese emperor to the west and to the lord of the Satsuma fief to the north in Japan.

The overlords of the Ryukyu kingdom decreed there should be no weapons in the islands. No swords. No spears. No matchlocks. Nothing even remotely resembling a weapon. So the Ryukyu people learned to fight and protect themselves with their bare hands, sticks, and small pieces of steel that looked not at all like weapons. They developed a system called kara ti. The word meant 'hand of China' because it had roots in Chinese methods of kung fu and tai chi chuan. Kara ti was a deadly art and the Oriental Shoo Lee was a master of it.

When the sun peeped over the horizon east of Diablo, often the only thing that moved was a single figure, barefooted and bareheaded, with a rolled bandanna tied around his head as a sweatband.

No one paid any attention to the Chinaman Shoo Lee as he danced among the rocks above Canyon Diablo. They didn't care if he spent an hour, sometimes two, moving through his kara ti positions time after time, engraving them on his subconscious so his body acted and reacted without conscious thought.

After working with kara ti, Shoo Lee set up a two-by-twelve plank of ponderosa pine and thumped it with his fists, taking care that his arms were straight from shoulder to knuckles. He'd soon need a new board as his knuckles had chewed nearly an inch into the one he was using.

Shoo Lee didn't think of Butch Kennedy at all. He merely continued his daily routine. When the sun rose high enough, he went with pigtailed Chinamen to the open space next to Hall's warehouse where laborers waited for hire. White men got paid a dollar for a job and the rest — the Chinese, the blacks, the Indians, the Mexicans — got half as much. Not because they asked for less or did less labor, but because the white men paying for the work decided they were worth less. That made Irishmen mad, because cheap Chinamen and other men of color got all the work when jobs were scarce.

The day after Samuel Jones set up the fight with Butch Kennedy, there were no jobs. The train was late. The stage was late. And Shoo Lee saw no

41

reason to stay in a vacant lot where the hot sun reflected off the red sandstone and black malapai rocks. The railway roadbed offered a halfway decent place to run, so Shoo Lee left the Chinamen, blacks, and Mexicans who stood around in hopes of an odd job, and strode down Hell Street. He noticed the line of men in front of Poker Flat, but thought nothing of it.

One of the men in the line pointed at Shoo Lee. 'Hey! There's the Chinaman Butch Kennedy's gonna kill.'

Shoo Lee went on as if he'd not heard the shout. He'd found it often worked better if people thought he didn't understand English well, but nearly five years in Yuma prison and more than a dozen years on tramp steamers before that had taught him a lot more English than he let on. In prison, his cellmate, Shawn Brodie, had even taught him to read and write.

'Hey, Chinaman.'

Shoo Lee walked on.

'Hey!' A shot sounded and a bullet

nicked the road ahead of Shoo Lee and whined off up the track.

Shoo Lee halted, but did not turn to face the heckler.

'You Chink shit. Butch's gonna clean your Chinky ass, you know. If you don't get shot first, uppity bastard.'

Shoo Lee slowly turned to face the man with the gun in his hand. He bowed deeply, hands steepled as the southern Chinese did.

'Thank you so much for warning me, sir. You are so very kind. If you please, I must run away along the railroad tracks. I must gather my strength before I meet Mister Butch in six more days. If you please, sir.'

Mollified, the would-be gunman shoved his revolver back into his waistband. 'Just so's you know your goldam place around here. No Chinee's gonna get uppity, else I'll shoot the bastard.'

Shoo Lee bowed deeply again. 'By your leave, sir,' he said.

The man waved a hand like shooing

away flies. 'Get outta here,' he said. 'Gotta bet to place.' He laughed like he thought Shoo Lee had bowed to a greater power.

Shoo Lee trotted away, headed out of town to run along the track roadbed in his bare feet — ten miles out, ten miles back. Endurance was important in a fight, and Shoo Lee kept his up by running twenty miles three times a week, sometimes four.

Just past the ten-mile mark, the A&P tracks passed over a small trestle and through a cut. He saw boulders piled on the tracks. It looked like someone had dynamited part of one side of the cut so it would make the train stop. It wouldn't be the first time the A&P train had been held up, but it looked like more than just a hold-up for whatever valuables the passengers might be carrying. Shoo Lee picked up his speed, then slowed down again. Why should he help the A&P, or any other white man for that matter? When had any white man been fair to him? When, since he'd been cell mates with Shawn Brodie? Shoo Lee wondered for a brief instant where Shawn might be.

Far up the track a train's whistle blew. Then Shoo Lee could hear the engine's chuffing. Coming fast. Perhaps too fast to brake to a stop before it plowed into the fallen boulders that lay around a curve in the tracks. The only way to save the train was to get far enough beyond the boulders and the trestle to flag it down. Shoo Lee sprinted along the tracks, dodged through the boulders, and turned on an additional burst of speed, running between the rails with his feet hitting every other tie. He pounded over the trestle and on to the far bank, still going full out. A hundred yards. Two. Three. He made out the oncoming steam engine with its train of cars.

Apparently the engineer saw him too, because the train's steam whistle gave a long howl.

Shoo Lee stripped his shirt off and waved it back and forth as he ran. The farther from the boulder barricade he could get, the better chance the train would have to stop. He waved and ran and hoped the engineer wouldn't just run over a Chinaman.

* * *

The engineer must have decided something was wrong if a man was sprinting up the tracks waving a shirt over his head. The screech of steel on steel sounded as the locomotive brakes went on. Then the engineer put the big drive wheels into reverse.

Shoo Lee slowed and stopped, but he kept waving his shirt like a warning flag.

The train came on. Sparks flew from the rails as the drive wheels thundered in reverse. It wouldn't stop before Shoo Lee, but maybe before the trestle. When the engine closed to a dozen feet, Shoo Lee nimbly leapt aside and sprang up into the cab as it passed.

'What the . . . a goldam Chinaman,' shouted the engineer. His hand moved to disengage the brakes.

Shoo Lee matched the engineer's shout. 'Barricade ahead. Boulders across the tracks just past the trestle. Honorable sirs.'

'No. Shit! Good thing we're stopping. Good thing.' The engineer set his face in a stubborn frown and peered ahead, trying to see around the bend.

'Yes, sir. Maybe bad men want to rob your train, too,' said Shoo Lee. 'Is there a way to warn the guards and the conductor?'

The engineer threw a glance at Shoo Lee. Then shook his head. 'No way in hell,' he shouted.

'I shall go.' Instants later, Shoo Lee scrambled over the coal tender and jumped up on top of the first car. He struggled back into his shirt as he ran. He cursed himself as well, as he remembered all the slights and sneers he'd gotten from white men and how white women pretended he wasn't there at all. He ran.

Shoo Lee dropped into the vestibule

of the first car and threw open the door. A glance showed him two cowboys, a drummer, and a woman with blonde hair done up in ringlets. He assumed she was a back-East girl.

'Barricade ahead, just across the trestle. Maybe a robbery so keep your guns handy,' Shoo Lee shouted. He climbed up on the second passenger car and repeated his warning.

Next came the baggage car. If there were anything worth stealing, it would be in that car, and the robbers would have plenty of time to blow the safe because they were too far from Diablo for the noise of shooting or explosions to reach town and bring curious people running down the track.

He lay flat on the roof over the door and pounded it with his fist.

'Who in hell is out there?'

Shoo Lee didn't bother identifying himself. 'Barricade ahead,' he roared. 'May be a hold-up.'

'Barricade? Holdup?'

'That's what I said. Keep your guns

loaded and cocked until the train starts rolling again.'

'Dunno who you are, but we're always ready.'

Shoo Lee made his way across a flat car loaded with lumber and a freight car that probably carried supplies for Diablo and surrounding ranches. Some would get hauled to Flagstaff and towns west as well.

At last he reached the caboose and lowered himself to the rear platform. The conductor already stood there, peering ahead as if to make out why the train was making an emergency stop. He whipped around as Shoo Lee landed, knees slightly bent and left hand splayed, palm toward the conductor.

'Barricade ahead, sir,' Shoo Lee said. 'Someone blew out one side of the cut and there's rocks three, four feet deep across the rails. Robbery, I'd say.'

'Shit.'

Shoo Lee nodded.

'Better set the brakes. Wondered why

we were slowing down like that.' The conductor shoved his head into the caboose and hollered. 'Ed. Ed Scheindekker. Get your lazy butt out here and set the car brakes.'

A goliath of a man came out the door sideways. 'I hear you, Ron. No need to shout like I was deef or something.'

'Set the brakes. Start with the caboose and work forward.'

The brakeman scrambled atop the car with the agility of a much smaller man. He twirled the brake wheel and the train's momentum dropped. The brakeman moved forward and set the brakes on the next car. And the next. The train slowed to walking speed, and just before moving on to the trestle it came to a complete stop. It stood there, steam escaping through open cocks, hissing like some storybook monster.

Shoo Lee and the conductor walked down the track to the locomotive. The engineer stuck his head out of the cab and called, 'Whaddaya figure, Ron?'

The conductor just waved a hand

and continued up the track to the trestle. The track curved as it left the trestle, so the conductor could not see the barricade of boulders from where he stood in front of the train.

'Can't see the barricade from here,' the conductor said. 'Need to get a look at it.' He spoke to himself as much as to Shoo Lee, who'd kept pace with him.

'Perhaps it could be dangerous on the other side,' Shoo Lee said.

'Need to have a look,' the conductor repeated. 'Need to know how much of a crew to send to clean the debris off the tracks.'

'I can clean it up,' Shoo Lee said. 'One hundred dollars.'

'You and what army?'

'Me and lots of Chinamen,' Shoo Lee said.

'How long? A day?'

'Two, maybe.'

The conductor considered Shoo Lee's offer. 'Still need to have a look-see,' he said, and started across the trestle.

Shoo Lee followed. There was nothing else he could do. White men didn't listen to Chinamen anyway, no matter that Shoo Lee himself was not from China.

They crossed the trestle without incident, but when they rounded the curve and could see the barricade, four men armed with rifles stood in a human barricade across the tracks in front of a slide of stone that covered the roadbed and the rails.

'Keep right on coming,' one of the men called. They had eyes for the conductor only. No one paid any attention to Shoo Lee. Everyone knew that one white man was worth a dozen Chinamen in a scrap, no problem.

The conductor resumed his trek toward the rockslide. Shoo Lee followed. If he could just get close enough . . .

'I'm Ronald Wilkinson,' the conductor said. 'I am on railroad business. I need to inspect the stone barricade that has been thrown across A&P tracks.'

'The hell you say.'

'Please stand aside, gentlemen,' Wilkinson said.

The talkative one worked the lever on his rifle, a Winchester Yellow Boy that showed considerable hard use. 'My buddy Mr Winchester here says you stand still, Mr Railroad Man.'

Shoo Lee moved off to the right a couple of steps. No one followed his movement with a rifle.

The conductor walked on with stolid steps. Perhaps he expected the hold-up man to blast him with the cocked Winchester. Perhaps he didn't care.

The talkative man screeched out his warning. 'Hold it!'

Wilkinson smiled. 'Are you going to kill me for attending to railroad business?' he asked.

'You'd better goldam believe it!' The hold-up man's answer was still closer to a screech than to speech from a man in control of himself. Wilkinson kept walking, affecting nonchalance, but Shoo Lee could see he was wound as tight as a pocket watch spring.

The man with the Yellow Boy pulled its trigger. The bullet slammed into the roadbed and wined off into the distance. 'Stop, I said.' The man still screeched.

'Did you men blow the cut?' Wilkinson asked.

'Damn right we did.' The same man spoke for the group.

Nearly close enough. Shoo Lee sidled another half step to the right. All four men had their eyes on Ron Wilkinson.

Shoo Lee palmed a throwing-star, which looked like a four-pointed spur rowel. Thrown correctly, it could bury any one of its points two inches into a pine board.

'And what do you expect to accomplish?' Wilkinson asked. He'd come to a stop face to face with the talker, who took an involuntary step back.

The spokesman held his rifle aimed at Wilkinson's midriff. He took his right hand off the action and wiped it on the leg of his threadbare canvas trousers.

He puffed out his chest. With his finger again on the trigger, he said, 'You all just turn back around and march right back up the tracks to that there train and we'll follow along.' He took a deep breath. 'An' when we gets there, you all can hand over what's in the baggage car. All the cash, y'hear?'

Wilkinson laughed.

The spokesman sputtered. 'Sumbitch. I'm gonna just kill you dead.' He raised the old Winchester to his shoulder and shut one eye.

Shoo Lee sent the throwing-star flying toward the spokesman with a flick of his right hand. He didn't wait to see where the star hit, he took a step forward, did a jumping turn, and smashed the edge of his horn-hard left foot into the larynx of the man to the spokesman's left.

Wilkinson stepped back in reaction. Shoo Lee seemed to flow across the tracks in front of the A&P man. He landed with legs spread, left foot slightly in front of the right, left hand out with fingers spread, right fist doubled next to his ribs. With a hoarse shout, Shoo Lee sent his right fist into the chest of the third man, smashing the first two knuckles into his sternum.

The man's eyes bulged. His tongue protruded. He dropped like an ear-shot hog and didn't move.

Shoo Lee was already whirling to his right. He took a step closer to the last man and smashed his right fist into the side of the man's face. The man staggered. Shoo Lee's left instep found his gonads and crushed them up against his pelvis. The man collapsed and began to gag on his own vomit.

'Save one,' Shoo Lee said. 'Tell who the robbers are.'

Wilkinson took another good look at the downed men. The spokesman lay still where he'd collapsed, the throwing-star protruding from his temple. The man with the crushed larynx drowned in his own bile. The one Shoo Lee had struck in the chest lay on his back, spread-eagled, eyes open to the sky.

'One hundred dollars,' Shoo Lee said, waving at the pile of rocks lying across the tracks. 'Two days.'

4

Before dawn, Shawn Brodie was out of the bunk he'd slept in at the far end of the Lazy EP bunkhouse. He didn't exactly creep out, but he took care not to make any extra noise. A light showed in the kitchen, so Shawn stuck his head in.

'Coffee ain't ready,' said a wrinkled old man.

'That you, Talltale?' Shawn said. 'You outta Yuma already?'

'Well I'll be hornswaggled. If it ain't pretty boy Shawn Brodie. What in heaven's name'r you doing at the Lazy EP? Oh, an' no one here calls me Talltale. I go by Gabby. Got that?'

Shawn grinned. 'Sure thing, Gabby. I come to see if you had enough wood for the stove.'

'Always room for another armload of wood. Should be some split up out at

58

the woodpile. Couple of armloads'd be good.'

'I'll get 'em,' Shawn said. 'Then we can think about some coffee.'

'Know where the woodpile is? Pretty dark out there.'

'Nope.'

'Just walk straight away. You'll stumble over it.'

'Gotcha.' Shawn turned his back to Gabby Talltale's kitchen and walked due west by the stars. He'd gone only about a hundred paces when dark stacks of cord wood showed a little to his right. A single-bit axe stuck in a great hunk of pitch pine showed him where the split pieces were. He took time to go through one set of kara ti exercises before he loaded up with split and kindling and carried it back to the wood box outside Gabby's kitchen. He placed the wood properly and went back for another load. But before he loaded up, he went through another set of exercises. One more armload, one more set of exercises, and Shawn put his head in the kitchen door again.

'Full up, Gabby,' he said. 'Any chance the coffee's perked?'

'You hang on, young'un. Coffee in two shakes of a dead lamb's tail.' Gabby cackled at his own joke.

Shawn sat down on the stoop.

Dawn was just turning on the lights and the surrounding country showed in shades of blue when Guy Rankin came out of the bunkhouse. He rubbed his eyes, yawned, and went to the washstand to splash cold water on his face. He dried with a piece of old flour sack hanging on a nail. Stropping the straight razor, Rankin examined his face in the bit of mirror tacked above the washbasin before chopping off the few whiskers between his sideburns and his moustache and goatee. He splashed his face again, took another swipe with the flour sack, and strode toward the kitchen, adjusting his hat as he came.

''Morning, boss,' Shawn said. He moved over so Rankin could mount the steps.

'See you got coffee,' Rankin said.

'An' he filled the goldurn woodbox, too,' Gabby said from inside. 'More'n you cowpokes do.'

'Our job's looking after Mr Peel's beeves, Gabby, not hauling wood for your damned stove.' Rankin chuckled. 'You got on Gabby's good side, Brodie. Could be worth a extry egg for you.'

'I got new coffee, boss. That's good to me.'

'An' here's a cup for you,' Gabby said. He shoved a stoneware mug into Rankin's hands.

'Obliged, Gabby.' Rankin sucked in equal amounts of air and hot coffee. 'Damn,' he said. 'Ain't nothing like a good hot cuppa coffee first thing in the morning.'

'Thanks to Shawn Brodie, Cap,' Gabby said. 'He brung the wood.'

Rankin sent a sharp glance Shawn's way. 'You know Brodie, Gabby?'

'Do I know Brodie? I was right there when he saved the warden from them crazy Mexes what tried to break out of the Hell Hole. And Shawn with no gun, Cap. No gun atall.'

'You talk too much, Gabby,' Shawn said. 'Just like always.'

Rankin narrowed his eyes, but he didn't pry. 'Reckon filling up Gabby's woodbox earned you breakfast, Brodie. We'll talk about other stuff later.'

Gabby stepped out the kitchen door and clanged a steel triangle with a hammer hanging from a piece of rope that looked like a piggin string.

Cowboys boiled from the bunkhouse and lined up at the washstand. A splash and a swipe did for most of them. Two stopped long enough to use the straight razor. Red and Brick were there along with the other cowboy who'd never said his name. Shawn'd slept in the far bunk of eight in the bunkhouse. One other had been empty, one unslept in.

'Come'n get it,' Gabby shouted, 'else I'll throw it out.'

Shawn waited until all five cowboys were seated. Rankin called Shawn. 'Get in here, Brodie.'

'Obliged,' Shawn said. He sat on the end of the bench.

'Hats off,' Rankin said. 'Hat in hand,' he added. 'God. Thanks for the food. Amen.' He clapped his hat back on and reached for a platter of sausage patties. 'Help yourselves,' he said.

Sausages, fried eggs, saleratus biscuits, thick gravy, hot coffee — there was no sign of money trouble at the Lazy EP. Shawn ate lightly. He didn't like a heavy stomach in the morning.

About the time the Lazy EP riders had finished their meal, a horse pounded up to the ranch house.

'Yow wee,' came a rebel yell. A cowboy crashed into the kitchen, red-faced and a little unsteady on his legs.

'Sheesh, Hansen. You smell like shit warmed over. You know enough to get back in time to sleep it off.' Rankin's voice carried a sharp edge.

The cowboy Hansen ignored the foreman. 'Heee hooo. Y'all wanna make a killing? Double? Triple your money?

I'll tell you what. A week from yesterday, there's gonna be a big fight in Diablo. The mick Butch Kennedy's gonna fight some Chinee asshole half his size. Bare knuckles. No holds barred. Odds ain't all that good, but there ain't no way Kennedy ain't gonna pound that shit-eating Shoo Lee or whatever his name is into little pieces.'

Gabby looked at Shawn. Shawn looked at Gabby. Together they gave a little shake of their heads. They'd not tell the Lazy EP crew the truth about Shoo Lee, if that's who the Chinaman was.

'Damn it, Hansen. No breakfast for you. Hit the bunkhouse and sleep it off. I'll talk with you tonight.' Rankin turned his attention to the other cowboys. 'Brick, you and Red go with Billings and Haycock over toward the crater. Push anything you find over to the corrals at Turner Flat. You can brand dogies there.'

'Gotcha, boss,' the men chorused. They left their plates on the table as they scrambled to get their mounts and equipment ready for the day.

Shawn stood up and started collecting plates and silverware, meaning to take them to the kitchen sink.

'Brodie?'

'Yeah, boss.' Shawn kept moving, clearing up for Gabby.

'Whatcha doing, boy?'

Shawn stopped, his face hard. 'You're the boss and I respect that, Rankin. But you ain't got no call to talk down to me. I'm just doing my share.' He walked over to the sink and deposited the dirty dishes there. He turned back to Rankin, his face still hard.

Rankin didn't meet his eyes. 'Sorry,' he murmured. He cleared his throat. 'You saw what shape Hansen was in. What would you say to riding with me to check the line over toward Winslow?'

'Working?'

Rankin nodded.

'That's what I came looking for.'

'Dollar a day and found,' Rankin said. 'But Mr Peel will have to say if you can stay on permanent like.'

'Good enough for me. You got a remuda horse for me? General could do with some rest.'

'You got anything against pacers?'

'Long as it's got hair, I can ride it.'

'Then you take the big bay in the far corral. He's got lots of bottom. Name's Pocoueno.'

The bay proved docile, easily caught by merely walking up to him in the corral. Rankin gave Shawn a bridle from the tack room that he said Pocoueno was used to. The horse took the bit without protest and followed Shawn through the gate and around to where Shawn's saddle straddled a stall wall in the horse barn. He'd turned General into the paddock and now the big quarter horse rolled himself in the loose chaff where horses obviously liked to roll.

'General,' he called. The horse's head came up as he regained his feet. 'You be good. Rest up.' Shawn hauled the saddle off the stall wall and shook out the blanket. He held the blanket so Pocoueno could get a good whiff of it, and tossed it on to the bay's back. Where some horses would have shied, Pocoueno stood still, head up and ears pricked.

'You'll do, old son,' Shawn said, 'if you've got as much bottom as you've got nerve.' Pocoueno swung his head around and bumped Shawn on the backside as he heaved the saddle up on to the horse's back. The saddle landed right, but Shawn had to take a step to keep from falling. Pocoueno gave him an innocent stare. Shawn laughed.

'OK. OK. I'll pay attention to what I'm doing.'

He settled the blanket and saddle and reached under to bring the surcingle to the onside. He fitted the latigo through the cinch ring and back up over the front dee ring for three turns, then tightened it up. He could tell Pocoueno was inflating his barrel and holding it tight so the cinch would go loose when he let all the air out.

Shawn punched him in the barrel.

'Give up the air, old son,' he said, with mock severity. 'You really don't want me to fall off halfway between here and Winslow, do you?' He took the reins and made Pocoueno quickly switch ends three times, then tightened the cinch again. He put the tail of the latigo through the tie strap holder and shook the saddle. It was on firm.

'You're gonna have to get a whole bunch smarter to pull the wool over my eyes,' Shawn said. He looped Pocoueno's reins over the corral fence and went to fill his canteen at the well pump. The water was cool and tasted good when Shawn cupped a hand for a mouthful. Not salty like Joe City water. With the canteen hung on his saddle, Shawn rode over to the big house where Rankin waited.

'You handle that stubborn gentle cayuse pretty good,' Rankin said.

'I ain't got a lariat,' Shawn said. 'We gonna need one?'

'Better have one,' Rankin said. 'Never can tell what's gonna happen.'

'Borrow one?'

'Tack room.'

Shawn reined the bay around toward the tack room, where he found a good rawhide reata that he hooked to his saddle horn opposite the canteen.

Back at the house, he hollered at Rankin. 'I'm ready, boss.'

Rankin came out with two packages in his hands. He tossed one at Shawn. 'Vittles,' he said. 'Never can tell when you'll need them.'

Shawn caught the pack and shoved it in the onside saddlebag. 'Thanks,' he said.

Rankin took the trail back to the calf pens, then lined out along the Little Colorado. Lazy EP basically stayed south of the river, but owned little patented land. But then, neither did the Hashknife. The A&P railroad got every other section for forty miles each side of the track and often sold the land for a few cents per acre.

Outfits like Hashknife and Lazy EP bought a few sections, which allowed them to control many more.

As they rode, Rankin and Shawn kept an eye out for Lazy EP stock. They saw none.

'Oughta be cows around here,' Rankin said. 'We ain't gathered these parts since spring.' He kept his eye on the ground as they rode, and eventually pulled up where marks on the ground showed that a bunch of cows, some with calves, had been driven past.

'Nobody oughta be driving no cows around here,' Ranklin said as if musing to himself. 'Let's follow these tracks,' he said aloud, and reined his horse around.

Shawn rode Pocoueno off to one side, not wanting to add his hoofprints to the ones leading southeast. Now and then, he took a swig from his canteen. The water was good, even hours after he'd filled it.

Rankin pulled up. 'I think I know where these beeves're going,' he said.

'There's a little blind canyon just this side of Sunset Pass that's good for holding cows. Let's beeline for that canyon.'

They kicked their horses up to a working trot, or, at least Rankin's pony trotted. Pocoueno just stretched his legs a little, like a good pacer should, and Shawn didn't get the thumps to his backbone that trotting would have given him.

'They call it Piñon Canyon because there's piñons mixed in with cedars on the rim. Only one way in and one way out. Good place to hold cattle for a day or two.'

Shawn didn't say anything.

They heard the cows bawling long before they reached Piñon Canyon.

★   ★   ★

Samuel Jones sat at his assigned table in Poker Flat. Maisie, dressed in yellow silk and white lace, perched in a chair next to the upright piano, where a black

71

man called Willie Tinkle played for hours at a time. Keno Harry didn't like a quiet place. The more noise, the more the money flowed — that was Harry's commercial philosophy anyway.

'How did you come to play piano like that, Tinkle?' Maisie asked.

'Don't rightly know, Miss Maisie,' Tinkle said. 'Were you to hum me a tune right now, I'd just know what keys to plonk to make the pianny give out with your tune. Just happens that way.' Tinkle did a particularly complicated riff. 'Sometimes I just play the tunes in my head,' he said.

'I'll be damned,' Maisie said.

'Not by my pianny, you won't.' Tinkle laughed.

Maisie laughed. But the sound of laughter didn't get far in the noisy gambling joint.

Maisie noticed a tall slim man stop to watch Samuel shuffle and work his cards. A sheep? He looked more like a big rangy prairie wolf. *You be careful, Samuel Jones.*

'May I join you?' the wolfish stranger said.

'Why, certainly. Would you like to work the cards?' Samuel said. He always invited new participants to shuffle the deck so he could judge their skill.

The prairie wolf sat down.

'Samuel Jones.' Samuel pushed the deck across the table.

'Beau, they call me,' the man said. 'Short for Beauregard.'

'Well, Beau. What is your pleasure today?'

Beau shuffled the cards and cut the deck a couple of times. 'What should we play?' he asked. 'And what is the ante?'

Samuel saw him palm a card, but said nothing. Gambling was, after all, a game of skill. Samuel prided himself on playing a straight game, but that did not mean he was unaware of the tricks others tried.

'Your tongue seems to say you are a Southern man, Samuel. Would I be prying if I asked wherebouts?'

'Bayou country,' Samuel said. 'And riverboats. I reckon I've been up and down Ol' Miss more times than the Dixie Belle herself.' It wasn't the whole truth, but a man never tells the whole truth to a stranger, even if he is a professional gambler.

'Bayou country, eh? Hear they rassle caymans down there.' Beau shuffled again. The card he'd filched, or one like it, went back into the deck. No doubt he'd marked it somehow.

'Kids trying to prove they're tough do that,' Samuel said. 'Boy gets to be a man, he has no more proving to do, caymans or whatever.'

Beau nodded. 'See your point.' He slapped the deck on to the tabletop. '*Vingt-et-un*,' he said.

Samuel nodded. 'That's the one we call blackjack, right?'

'As if you didn't know,' Beau said. 'All Cajuns parley vous a little French. Frenchys they be.'

Samuel nodded. 'You could say that,

74

I suppose. My own grandfather was Arcadian. Blackjack, then?' He reached for the deck. 'My table. I'll deal.'

Beau nodded. 'So be it.'

Samuel narrowed his eyes. 'Before we start, let's get to the bottom of this. You didn't arrive in Diablo by chance, did you, Beau? And you didn't come to break the bank, or you'd be at the faro table. So what is it?'

The prairie wolf smiled only enough to show his fangs. 'I think you have met Valentine Hebert,' he said.

'I killed him,' Samuel said, and palmed his two-shot .41 Derringer beneath the table.

'That you did, sir,' Beau said. 'He bared you for who you are, Philippe Beaumont. Assassin and murderer.'

5

Shoo Lee didn't think about the coming fight with Butch Kennedy; he had a job to do. For a hundred dollars he was to clear the rails of rocks in two days. He insisted on half in advance, which he promised to a crew of twenty-five Chinese, Mexican, and black workers. He told them to take a roundabout way from Chinktown to the rock slide so that the Irish workers wouldn't find out about the job until too late.

Wilkinson took the train back to Winslow, where he'd wait for two days. If the tracks were clear when the train came through, Shoo Lee would get the second fifty dollars.

With Wilkinson went any knowledge of Shoo Lee's fighting skills. So rumors should not spread.

The workers got the best part of the

smaller rocks off the tracks and into the gorge by sundown the first day. When they trekked back into Chinktown by twos and threes Shoo Lee had food ready at Wai Hong's *dim sum* house, which was the best eatery in all Chinktown. He gave the workers all the rice they could eat, plus fried greens and tubers from Diablo Canyon and cow's stomach chopped and boiled tender, then flavored with garlic and soy sauce. The meal cost Shoo Lee two-fifty, but ten cents a head was nothing compared to the goodwill garnered for being so generous.

Hang Jolin, the taipan of Chinktown, sidled up to Shoo Lee. 'I hear you got a big job from the railroad,' he said in the singsong accent that the Cantonese affected.

'Not bad, sir,' Shoo Lee said. He palmed a tightly rolled ten-dollar bill and handed it to Hang. 'A small honorarium, sir.' He leaned close to Hang's ear. 'If you would like to increase that meager honorarium ten-fold, sir, go to Poker Flat and bet on me to beat the beefy Irishman Butch Kennedy.'

Hang kept a sober face, but his eyes sparkled at the thought of making money by doing nothing. 'Thank you for the gratuity, Shoo Lee. I see your country knows how to treat celestials as myself.'

'Of course, sir. Centuries of practice,' Shoo Lee said. 'By your leave.'

He ate sparingly of the *dim sum* Wai Hong had prepared, and went to his tarpaper shack at the edge of Chink-town. He carefully hid the remaining forty dollars of his advance. The following day, he would have to pay twenty-five to the workers at the end of the day, as he too had promised half. If the railway failed to make good on its promise, the workers would still make as much as usual. He stripped to his loincloth and began a series of stretch-ing exercises reminiscent of yoga. Finished, he sat in a lotus position and meditated, murmuring in a hollow monotone: *namuamidabutsu, namuamidabutsu, namuamidabutsu.*

He slept on a platform of planks covered with straw. He had no dreams.

Shoo Lee awoke some hours before dawn. He did three repetitions of his kara ti exercises, then stood in a one-legged heron pose on a rock high above Diablo Canyon. He stood motionless, waiting for the sun to rise. And when it poked its nose above the eastern skyline, Shoo Lee ate a single rice ball and ran toward the rockslide in his bare feet.

Shortly after Shoo Lee arrived at the rock slide, the other workers began coming in by twos and threes. The twenty-five-man crew consisted of thirteen Chinese, eight Mexicans, and four blacks.

'Hey, boss,' called a Chinese named Won Bailee. 'How we work today all?'

Shoo Lee divided them up into six-man teams. He saved the littlest Chinese to carry water. 'Your job is very important,' he said. 'Men must drink water to work hard.'

Two teams continued clearing up the smaller rocks, carting them to the trestle and dumping them into the river. Two teams went to work with ropes and levers, tumbling large rocks down the tracks, on to the trestle, and over the side into the gorge. Long before the sun reached the edge of the San Francisco peaks in the west, the A&P tracks were clear of debris.

A train's whistle sounded from up the tracks, and Wilkinson's locomotive came puffing across the trestle and into the cut. It came to a halt, steam valves hissing. Wilkinson stepped off the caboose and made his way to the front of the train.

Shoo Lee met him. The crews stayed back. 'Your track is clear, Mr Wilkinson,' Shoo Lee said.

'Well done. Well done indeed,' Wilkinson said. He reached into his leather wallet and withdrew a bundle of bills. 'Fifty dollars in ones, as you requested.' Wilkinson placed a double eagle on the top of the bundle. 'And twenty dollars more to you, extra, for a job well done.'

Shoo Lee bowed deeply. He palmed the gold coin and took the bundle of greenbacks. 'It was a privilege to work for you, Mr Wilkinson. When difficult jobs need done quickly, ask for Shoo Lee, please.'

Wilkinson laughed. 'That I will. That I will. The railroad always needs someone who comes through, someone who says what he means and means what he says.'

Shoo Lee stepped a little closer to Mr Wilkinson and spoke in a low voice. 'In four days there will be a fight in Diablo,' he said. 'Myself, Shoo Lee, must fight with a large Irishman named Butch Kennedy. I will beat him, Mr Wilkinson. You can bet a wager on that. I am smaller. I am older, but I shall beat him quite severely, I fear. If you have some extra money, I suggest you go to the gambling house called Poker

Flat and make your bet.'

The train blew its whistle. 'Come on, Mr Wilkinson. We ain't got all day,' yelled the engineer. The steam valves hissed and the engine chugged and the drive wheels began to turn. Shoo Lee and Mr Wilkinson stood out of the way. The engineer kept the train at dead slow to make it through the cut. As the caboose neared, Wilkinson stepped up on to the rear platform. He waved a perfunctory hand toward Shoo Lee, then disappeared into the caboose.

'OK,' Shoo Lee shouted, 'line up by teams. Water boy, you out front.'

The teams lined up.

'Come to me, one at a time.'

They came, and Shoo Lee handed each man two dollars for two days' work. Last of all he handed the water boy two dollars as well. 'That's for keeping the other men from getting thirsty. A man cannot work without enough water.'

They wanted to whoop and shout. Shoo Lee knew that they wanted to.

'Don't celebrate loudly,' he said. 'Better if too many don't learn of your good fortune. Tonight's meal at Wai Hong's is on me again.'

The men slipped away, once again moving in twos and threes in roundabout ways back to Chinkburg.

Shoo Lee ran down the track bed, toughening his horn-hard feet as he went.

* * *

'Boss,' Shawn called.

Rankin reined in. 'Whatcha want, kid?'

'You reckon we oughta just go riding in on those cows?'

'Got a better idea?'

'Why don't I go first? People in this neck of the woods don't know me, and I seen that Pocoueno wears an H-Cross brand. You get him from Garet Havelock?'

'Don't know, rightly. Don't much matter around here.' Rankin thought for a moment. 'So what do you figure to do by going in first?'

'Maybe, if there's riders in there, maybe they'll let me in close, if I act like I'm riding the grubline.'

'So what?'

'So maybe I could take care of them.'

'You ain't even got a gun, a short one anyway. Left your Yellow Boy at the ranch, too. Sounds kinda dumb to me. Then again, I ain't got no better ideas.'

'OK. I'll ride in. You stay out of sight until I come back for you. If I can. If I can't, then you might want to get more riders before you come stomping in.' Shawn kicked Pocoueno and set a course for the open end of Piñon Canyon. When he passed the outlying rocks, he began to whistle *When I Was a Cowboy*. He didn't worry too much about making sure all the notes were exactly right.

The trail of the bunch of cattle they'd followed went into Piñon Canyon, no two ways about it. He whistled louder.

Brush grew down all the way to the wash at the bottom of the canyon, and the trail narrowed. Hoofprints of shoed horses chousing the cows stood out. There had to be someone in there with them. Shawn whistled, and reined Pocoueno along the cow path.

As Pocoueno pushed through the last of the one-seed junipers Shawn heard someone jack a shell into a Winchester. He kept whistling and rode slumped in the saddle like he was worn out and really hungry.

'Come in real careful, cowboy,' a voice said.

Shawn pushed his hands up and said, 'Hang on there, I'm real friendly. I seen them cow tracks and thought there might be something to eat for a down-and-out rannie like me.'

A young man in canvas pants, a muslin shirt, and a dark blue vest stepped out from behind a bush. His '73 Winchester was pointed at Shawn's chest. 'Where you from?'

'Grant's Crossing. Looking for work.

Well, right now I'm looking for a strip of bacon or maybe a biscuit if you've got one handy.'

As Shawn talked, Pocoueno ambled further into the canyon.

'Hey! Hey! You'd better stop that long-legged cayuse if you don't want me to plug him dead.'

'Got my hands in the air. Can't pull on the reins,' Shawn said.

'Well, put 'em down and stop the damn horse.'

Shawn did as he was told. The young man walked over to stand right in front of Pocoueno. He stared at Shawn.

'I'll be Shawn Brodie,' Shawn said. 'Recently from Grant's Crossing, and Yuma before that.'

'Yuma? What for?'

'They said I stole a cow.'

'No shit.' The rifle seemed to lower a little.

'Got any coffee?' Shawn said. 'You all by yourself?'

'Coffee? Nah. Ain't even got a fire.'

Shawn said, 'Hey, I ain't even got a

gun. Sold it in Holbrook. Needed food worse'n lead.'

'Mighty good saddle fer someone down and out.'

'It was on the horse.'

'No shit.'

'By yourself?'

'Yeah. But my buddies'll be back any minute.'

'Yeah? Can I get down while we wait for 'em? Will they bring any coffee? Something to eat?'

'Shut up a minute, wouldja? I can't think straight with all the talking going on.'

'OK if I get down?' While he talked, Shawn also got a good look at what was going on. The rustlers had separated cows from calves, putting the babies in a pen-like affair that backed up against the canyon wall and was made mostly of brush. Separation made the mama cows low for their offspring, but it also kept them from wandering off.

'You got any water?' Shawn asked.

'Shit. I ain't got nothing but this here

gun, and it's plumb full of bullets.'

Shawn unwound the strap of his canteen from the saddle horn. 'This water's pretty good. No alkali. Better'n Little Colorado mud by a long shot. Want some?'

The man with the Winchester licked his lips. 'Well . . . '

'I'm getting down,' Shawn said. 'Don't you shoot me.'

'Awright, but no funny stuff.'

Shawn dismounted and left Pocoueno ground tied. 'You never did say who you was,' he said.

'Ollie. Ollie Howard,' the man said, his eyes fastened on the canteen.

'Well, Ollie,' Shawn held out the canteen, 'it ain't Old Potrero or nothing fancy. Just plain old water.'

Ollie let the rifle slip into the crook of his arm as he reached for the canteen.

When Ollie's hand was almost ready to grab the canteen, Shawn dropped it, took a hold on Ollie's wrist, and threw him over his hip in a kara ti move something like a Flying Mare. Ollie let go of the Winchester as he flew through the air and smashed to the ground on his back. He lay there, dazed, as Shawn picked up the Winchester. He checked the action as Ollie lay there, groggy.

'Ollie? Ollie? You hear me?' Shawn said. He jabbed Ollie with the muzzle of the rifle. 'You hear me?' he said again.

'What the hell did you toss me for?' Ollie looked at the rifle in Shawn's hands, the whites of his eyes showing like a frightened colt's.

'Ollie. Listen to me. Ollie? You hear what I say?'

Ollie pouted. 'I hear you. What?'

'I ride for the Lazy EP, Ollie, and them's our cows. Now, I'm figuring you ain't no cow-thief. So have a drink from the canteen, then hightail it outta here before my boss comes.'

Ollie fumbled at the canteen's cork. Then he left it without drinking. 'Don't want water from no cheater,' he said.

'Your hide, Ollie. You got one chance. No way you can ride outta here without my boss catching you. Take to the hills. Climb out of the canyon and go wherever you want. Just don't let me catch you holding Lazy EP cattle in a box canyon again, y'hear?'

Ollie stood up. 'Yuma, my ass,' he said.

'I was at Yuma for nearly two years. In there, you steal someone else's stuff, you end up in solitary. Not fun. Now. If you don't want a drink, take a beeline for the cliffs and climb your way outta here.'

Ollie wiped his mouth with the back of his hand.

'I didn't kill you, Ollie. By rights, I could. Now get outta here.' Shawn shifted the rifle so it pointed at Ollie's gut. 'Can't miss from this close,' he said. 'Git.'

Ollie turned and ran toward the canyon wall. Shawn followed him with the muzzle of the Winchester until he'd actually begun climbing out of the canyon. He went to the brush calf-pen and pulled enough juniper away to let the calves get through. In minutes the dogies all sucked cow teats and bunted at their mama cows when the flow didn't satisfy them.

Shawn found Ollie's pinto horse tied to a scrub oak thicket. He untied it and led it as he started the cows moving toward the mouth of the canyon.

Rankin joined him soon after the cows got through the thick brush. He rode up close and said, 'Where'd you get the rifle and extry horse?'

'Rannie named Ollie give them to me, sort of.'

'Where's Ollie?'

'Well, you see, Ollie's not too bright and I don't think he oughta get strung up for stealing our cows. I gave him a head start. He left the rifle and the horse. Said his partners would be back soon, but he didn't stay around to see.'

'We push these cows a little, they'll naturally go back to their home range,' Rankin said. 'What if we was to wait for them rustlers to come back?'

Shawn shook his head. 'No telling

how many'll come, boss.'

'Yeah, but we'd have the drop.'

'Ollie had the drop, but I talked to him and then took his gun away. The drop ain't always the whole story.'

'Yeah, but I hate to let rustlers make off with our cows. They ain't no law in this territory. County sheriff's too far away. We gotta stomp out our own fires,' Rankin said.

'You trust me, boss?'

Ranklin took a very long look at Shawn's face. 'I reckon I do, Shawn.'

'Then you chouse them cows back on down the trail, and I'll stick around and find out who the rustlers are. OK?'

Rankin nodded. 'OK. But don't you get yourself kilt.'

Shawn handed Rankin the lead rope to Ollie's pinto. 'Wanna trade me rifles? Just in case there's something about Ollie's they might recognize?'

Rankin took Ollie's gun and passed his own over to Shawn. 'Hope this peashooter hits what I aim at.'

'Best not to have to shoot.'

Rankin reined his horse away and rode north toward Lazy EP range.

Shawn watched him for a while, then rode Pocoueno back into Piñon Canyon. He tied the bay to the scrub oaks where the paint had been, built a little fire, and sat down to see who would show up.

6

'Assassin and murderer?' Samuel said. 'Those are quite extreme words to use at a table where Lady Luck rules.'

Beau sneered. 'Since when is there honor at a gaming table?'

'Honor, sir, is something earned, not declared. Now.' Samuel left the cocked Derringer in his lap and shuffled the cards, quickly but fairly. He felt the mark on the card Beau had put back in the pack. He withdrew it and turned its face toward Beau.

'Sir, we both know this card is the deuce of clubs. I will replace it to the deck. When you get it, the mark will tell you, as it tells me when I deal it. If I get the card, however, you will not know. So as to not take unfair advantage of you, I will announce it whenever I have the deuce of clubs. Does that sound fair to you, Beau?'

'Very well.' Beau peeked at his cards. He matched Samuel's dollar with one of his own, then placed another in the pot.

'The last time I saw you, Philippe Beaumont, you were standing with a second, next to the dueling oaks in City Park, New Orleans.'

'Goodness. I've not been there for at least twenty years,' Samuel said.

'It would not surprise me if that day were your last day in the city. But, perhaps not. At any rate, you disappeared and no one has been able to find you.'

Behind Beau, Maisie sharpened her attention, feeling the tension between the two men at Samuel's table. She put down her drink and ambled over to where Pitch Duggan sat in a high seat overlooking the gaming area. He held a long-barreled 10-gauge, broke so anyone could see the big brass and red cartridges in the breech.

'Pitch, you keep your eye on that sumbitch with Samuel. He's carrying a chip on his shoulder that even I can see.'

Pitch snapped the shotgun closed. 'I'll watch,' he said.

Maisie wandered back and took her seat. Samuel never showed that he'd seen everything she did, but the skin around his eyes seemed to soften a bit. He put another dollar in the pot. And another.

'Matching and raising,' he said. 'City Park, eh? Not sure I remember such an occasion, Beau. Were you there for a picnic?'

Beau barked a laugh. 'A picnic at dawn? That would attract attention. No. That was the day young Larouche was shot by yourself on a trumped-up matter of honor.'

'Oh, really? If I am an assassin and murderer then, this young Larouche — is that his name? — Young Larouche is dead, is he not? Are you going to bet, Beau, or do you wish me to deal you another card?'

'Huh? Oh. Yes.' Beau peeked at his

cards and chewed his lips. 'One card, if you please,' he said.

Samuel dealt the card. 'So I supposedly assassinated this young Larouche, you say. If he were assassinated, then he must be long dead.'

Beau considered his cards and put a matching silver dollar in the pot. He turned his cards up. A king of hearts, a five of spades, and a four of diamonds.

'Nineteen,' Samuel said. 'A very good hand, Beau. Probably better than mine.' He turned his cards up. 'Ace of hearts for eleven and the eight of clubs for a total of nineteen. You take the pot, Beau, as ties go to the customer.' He pushed the silver dollars to the opposite side of the table.

Samuel gathered the two hands, put them aside, and dealt two cards to Beau and two to himself. Again he placed a silver dollar in the middle of the table. 'So what happened to young Larouche? How was I his assassin if he is not dead?'

'I survived, Philippe.'

For the first time, Samuel looked closely at the man who called himself Beau. 'André? André Larouche?'

The years had not been kind to Larouche. In New Orleans, he'd been debonair, dreamed of by many a young woman in the higher levels of society. Not rich, not rich at all, but with impeccable family lines, André Larouche.

'Are you going to continue the game?' Samuel asked.

'Oh. Yes. Of course.' Beau put a dollar in the pot and then raised a dollar. He'd not looked at his cards. He took a fine leather wallet from his inner coat pocket and extracted a folded paper. 'Here's what you said my life was worth to Delacorte.' Beau thrust the paper across the table.

Samuel picked it up and unfolded it, though he knew well what it was. 'You never cashed it, then?'

'Call me superstitious if you wish. You gave me my life in City Park that morning and paid for it. I've always felt that, if I were to cash that bank draft, I'd also be cashing in my own life. So now it's kind of a good luck charm.'

'Startling that I failed to recognize you, Beau.'

'What was I then? A stripling boy of sixteen who thought he was in love with the daughter of the Delacortes? I changed. You changed me.'

'I changed you?'

Beau nodded. The cards lay on the table, ignored. 'You showed me what a man's life was worth to those who stand in the upper echelons of society.'

'Here in Diablo two bits would buy your life, Beau. In fact, those shiny leather boots on your feet might be the price of your life to some poor bugger who's feet are cold.'

'The point is, there's always a price.'

Samuel raised an eyebrow. 'Didn't mean to turn you so cynical. Card?'

Beau looked at his cards, then at Samuel, who had yet to look at his own hand. 'I use Beauregard because of you,' he said. 'One card.'

Samuel dealt him one. 'How so?'

'You were Philippe Beaumont. I wanted a name that would remind me every day of what you gave me. Beau, as short for Beauregard, fit the role. What will you do? Match? Raise?'

Samuel rubbed his chin as if considering the card game. 'Can't figure why you'd come all the way to Diablo, Arizona, to say hello,' he said. He matched Beau with a dollar, then added a half eagle. 'I'll raise you five.'

Beau peeked at his three cards again. He put five silver dollars on the table. 'Match you. And call for one more card.'

Samuel dealt Beau a card. 'Can't figure why you're here. If you were hired by Delacorte you could stand back and shoot me with a long rifle.'

'Old man Delacorte is dead. Died shortly after you killed Hebert. Only one's hunting you now, as far as I know.'

Samuel finally looked at his own cards. He shrugged. 'Can't use any more cards,' he said. 'How about you?'

Beau shook his head. 'Too dangerous, playing with an assassin,' he said. 'But I will raise you.' He put a ten-dollar bill on the table.

'My, my,' Samuel said. 'True confidence.'

Beau's lips curved upward in what might have been a smile. It was too fleeting to tell for sure. 'True bombast, perhaps.'

'Bombast? The word alone is worth ten dollars.' Samuel laid out his two cards. A ten of diamonds and a nine of clubs.

Beau really did smile. He turned his cards over to show a six of hearts, a six of spades, and an eight of diamonds. 'Twenty,' he said. 'You just bought me dinner, Philippe.'

'Beau, you're aware that names out here may or may not be connected to former lives. My name is Samuel Jones, sometimes called Sam, most of the time, Samuel. Would you be so kind?'

Beau put his winnings away and left

the silver dollars on the table. 'Sure . . . Samuel,' he said.

'Thank you.'

'You all doing OK?' Pitch Duggan's 10-gauge filled the space between Beau and Samuel.

'Of course, Pitch. Thanks for asking. Meet Beau . . . ' Samuel raised his eyebrow toward Larouche.

'Bromwell,' Beau said. 'Beau Bromwell.'

'Beau knows a few of the same people I know,' Samuel said. 'Him being from bayou country.'

'Thass good,' Duggan said, and went back to sit on his lookout seat next to the bar.

'Samuel. There is one thing I know that might concern you.'

'Yes?'

'Old man Delacorte is dead. But Angélique is not. And she's hired Zeb Curtiss to find you and kill you.'

'Zeb Curtiss. Should I know him?'

'Probably not. He's a long-shooter. Doesn't get closer than a quarter of a mile, but shoots mostly from a half.'

'How do you come by this information?'

'You don't want to know,' Beau said. 'But I came to watch your back. I know you can take care of the close stuff, but Zeb's never gonna let you see him. Never at all.'

'And you'd be better? Than me, that is.'

'A whole bunch better.'

Samuel's eyebrows went up again. 'How so?'

Beau put his hands on the table and leaned forward. 'There was a time near the end of the recent unpleasantness when the Little Creole, my commander, put me in a tree and had me shooting Yankees for fun and entertainment. I can keep outta sight. And I know where to look for those who want to keep outta sight.'

'And you're just assuming I can't take care of myself?'

'Samuel, you've got a cocked Derringer in your lap. Anyone who tried something at this table would have that double-shot to deal with first, the sword in your cane second, the girl behind me third, and that cannon of a scattergun fourth.' Beau looked around. 'Yeah, you're fairly secure in here,' he said, 'but once you're out on Hell Street, you'll have nothing to stop the long bullet. That's where I come in.'

'Why?'

'Once you saved the life of a sixteen-year-old boy. He'd like to save yours.'

★   ★   ★

Shawn prayed. Not so much because he'd caught religion, but because he was sitting there by a fire that lit him up like some kind of turkey-shoot target. Times like this, he kinda wished he'd taken up smoking. Then he'd've had something to do with his hands.

Still, he heard the horses long before the riders got to his campfire. That, and Pocoueno stood at attention with his ears pricked at something coming up the canyon. Shawn took off his hat and let his blond hair hang down over his ears. He always looked younger that way.

Eyes closed to protect his night vision, Shawn sat face to the fire and listened. Two horses? No, three. Then the horses stopped. Shawn held his breath.

'Hey!'

Shawn made no move toward the rifle leaning against the log he sat on.

'Hey!'

'Hey yourself,' Shawn said, keeping his tone neutral.

'Whatcha doin'?'

'What does it look like? I just made me a camp. You got anything to eat? Last I ate was behind a widow's house in Winslow. She was throwing perfectly good food to a bunch of hogs.'

'She-it. Goldam grubline rider.'

'Gotta do whatcha gotta do. Don't ride the grubline, you end up dead on some corner in some town where no

105

one give a pickledy-piss about you.' Shawn knew he was rambling on, but people felt better when others rambled on like they was tetched a little.

'Hey!'

'Why you keep hollering like that?' Shawn shaded his eyes from the fire and peered into the dark every way but in the direction the riders came from.

'Where's our cows?'

'Cows? What cows?' Shawn had never sounded more innocent.

'They was fifty head of cows and baby calves here when we'uns left.'

'Nothin' when I came. Looked like a right safe box canyon, so I made me a camp. Ain't got no coffee, so I cain't offer you none. Would if I had some, though.'

'We're getting down. Don'chu do nothing funny. We got guns on you.'

'Come on in. Fire's all I got, but you all is welcome.' Shawn stood and hammers clicked.

'Whoa. Just standing up. It ain't proper to greet folks sitting down,'

Shawn said. 'My grandma in Kentucky always said that.' He stood slumped, arms hanging loosely.

Three men walked their horses up to Shawn's camp. All three had rifles and two had pistols, weapons that had seen more than their fair share of years. Not that Shawn was a firearms expert, but he knew a Joslyn side-hammer six-gun when he saw one. And two of the rifles were Yellow Boys that didn't have the shine of well cared-for weapons. The other rifle was a Henry, even older than the Yellow Boys, but looked after better.

'Sorry about the food problem,' Shawn said. 'And no coffee.' He didn't mention the grub in Pocoueno's saddle-bags.

'Where'd them cows go?' The speaker urged his ragged brown toward the fire.

'My name's Shawn Brodie,' Shawn said. 'I ain't seen no cows since I got here. But then, I ain't been here more'n a hour or so.'

'They was over there.' The man on

the brown pointed at the brush holding corral.

'Do I look like a man could hold a beef or two in there?' Shawn said. 'But I bet lots of folks use this canyon all the time.'

'Shit. Gone. Busted ass for two days. Gone. Damn.'

'You fellers work in these parts?' Shawn asked. 'I'd like to git some kinda riding job.'

'Uh? Us?' The man on the brown did all the talking. Maybe he was the brains. The others sat their horses with blank slack-jawed looks on their faces. Not bright, but that didn't mean not dangerous. Shawn remembered well how Robert Franklin, the man they called Goliath, had broken his arm, and Goliath hadn't meant to do it either.

'No cows here,' Shawn said. 'I ain't no tracker, but the tracks outta that ketch pen look purty fresh. Had me a buddy once who could tell how fresh tracks was by their smell. You ever tried that?'

'Damn. Gone. Ever' damn one of them gone.'

'I'm gonna put a stick on the fire,' Shawn said. 'Don't none of you shoot me.' He reached down, snagged a piece of juniper and laid it on the fire. The flames started right to work on it, and the fire got brighter. The men automatically pulled their horses back a step or two. Maybe they didn't want Shawn to see their faces.

'Whatcha gonna do?' Shawn asked. 'Kin I go along? I ride purty good. Not much of a hand with a rope, but OK riding.'

'Don't know y'all,' the boss man said. 'Got more men than I need anyways.' The riders hadn't let their hammer down. The rifles were fully cocked.

Shawn measured the distance to Rankin's rifle with his eyes. Then the distance to the ponderosa log on the far side.

The leader started to turn his horse away, but that brought his rifle to bear on Shawn. 'Now,' he shouted, and pulled the trigger.

But Shawn was gone. In his dive for the log he'd grabbed the '73 and cocked it as he flew through the air. The rifle and outstretched arms cushioned his fall and he rolled, coming up behind the log with the Winchester at his cheek. He tracked the leader for half a second and touched off a round. The man screamed and dropped from his horse like a sack of flour.

The other two frantically worked the levers of their guns, hoping to get bullets in the chambers before Shawn could shoot. But the action of Rankin's gun was smooth as buttered biscuit. Shawn had a bead on the bigger of the two almost as soon as the leader went down. He touched off another round and a second rustler fell flailing from his horse.

'Don't shoot! Don't shoot!' The third rider threw his Yellow Boy to the ground. 'I ain't armed. Don't shoot!'

Shawn stood up from behind the ponderosa log. He kept the Winchester to his cheek. 'Shed the hogleg,' he said.

The rider complied, using his left hand to take a pistol from his waistband and drop it to the ground.

'Git over here,' Shawn said.

The rider turned his horse back toward the fire. 'Don't kill me, mister.'

'Don't reckon to, but my boss might,' Shawn said. 'The law don't deal lightly with rustlers.' Shawn could see the third man more clearly now. He looked no more than twelve or thirteen years old. 'Get down off that poor excuse for a horse, kid,' he said, 'while I figure out what to do with you. You got a name?'

'Sylvester,' the kid said, 'but most people call me Sly.'

'I reckon them others that came with you are dead. Whatever possessed you to rustle Lazy EP cows? Dumbest thing I ever heard of.'

'Russ, he said it'd be easy like taking lollipops from a baby, that's what he said. There ain't no work in Diablo, and we needed' — the kid sniffled — 'and we was gonna die. Ellison Peel's as rich as Satan. He'd never miss a few cows. We got us some horses and we got a bunch o' cows 'n' put 'em in here with Ollie watching 'em.'

'Don't need your life's story, kid,' Shawn said. 'So you stole horses and rustled cows. Don't sound like something I'd want people in these parts to know. They hang thieves, don't they?'

The kid looked around. 'Where's Ollie? He was supposed to watch our cows.'

'Ollie took out. And the cows wasn't yours.'

'Jeez.'

'Yeah.'

The kid ducked his head and went to sniffling.

'Buck up, kid. When I was your age I got sent to Yuma Prison. Here I am. Ya just gotta be tough.'

The kid sniffled some more.

'Just get outta here,' Shawn said. 'Get that pony back to where no one will know he's been gone. Then maybe hop a freight to Winslow or Holbrook. Ya hear?'

'Me? Leave?'

'Yeah. Get out.'

'I ain't got no gun.'

'You're better off without one. Git!'

The kid sniffled again. Then there was silence in the canyon, except for the breeze coming down from the heights, rustling the junipers and scrub oaks on its way out to the flat. The kid turned his horse's head toward the canyon mouth and heeled it into motion.

Shawn stood for a long time, listening to the kid's horse pick its way out of the canyon. After the sound faded he loaded the rustlers belly down over their own saddles and tied them on. He doused the fire good, climbed aboard Pocoueno, and set out for the Lazy EP, leading two horses with dead men across their saddles.

7

Men in Chinkburg steepled their hands when they passed Shoo Lee. In a town that hired Chinese, Black, and Mexican labor only as an afterthought or as a way to get a job done cheaper, they saw Shoo Lee as a man who made the railway pay full wages for work done.

Shoo Lee stood at the edge of Canyon Diablo in a heron pose, his eyes closed and his breathing controlled and shallow. He'd completed his kara ti exercises and would do his ten mile run as soon as he'd quieted his body and mind.

'Shoo Lee. Shoo Lee!'

Shoo Lee maintained his heron pose.

'Shoo Lee!'

Footsteps pounded across the mala-pai and stopped in front of Shoo Lee. He held the pose for ten more breaths, then opened his eyes.

'What?' he said.

'Whiteman boss come look after you,' the Chinese youngster said.

'Speak English right, kid. You sound like a Chinaman.'

The youngster bowed. 'Whiteman boss wants to talk to you,' he said in his natural voice. 'He says he's from the Atlantic and Pacific Railway.'

'That's right. Well spoken. Only use your Chinaman accent when you need to play dumb. It gives you an advantage because white people assume you're not very smart when you speak like a Chinaman. Got it?'

The kid gave Shoo Lee a big grin. 'Got it,' he said. 'Come on. Let's go see what the whiteman boss wants. Everyone is curious.'

Shoo Lee relaxed his heron pose. 'OK. We'll go see.'

The whiteman boss turned out to be Wilkinson, the man who had hired Shoo Lee to clear the rocks off the track. He looked uncomfortable surrounded by people speaking three dialects of Chinese, Spanish, Cajun patois, and who knew what other language.

Shoo Lee steepled his hands and bowed as a Chinaman was expected to. 'Good morning to you, Mr Wilkinson. What brings you to Chinkburg, I wonder?'

'Ah. Shoo Lee. Good. Is there some place we can converse without all these people watching us?'

Shoo Lee thought for a moment. 'How private?' he asked.

'I don't want others to listen to our conversation, and I'd as soon not have people from Diablo know I was here.'

Shoo Lee's eyebrows rose. *Why all the secrecy?* 'Please come with me, Mr Wilkinson.' He took the rocky path that led to the Dream Chamber, an opium den run by Yu Wanglim, an entrepreneur from the Chinese province of Fukien.

'*Ho lei*, Wanglim?' he said at the entrance.

'*Ho*, Shoo Lee. What brings you

here? I have never seen you smoke poppy juice.'

'Of course,' Shoo Lee said. 'But I need a private room for a talk with this man. Private business.'

Wanglim gave Shoo Lee a knowing smile. 'Good girls, I know,' he said.

Shoo Lee shook his head. 'No. Business talk.'

'Okey dokey. Come. One dollar now. One dollar every hour.'

Wilkinson extracted a silver dollar from his vest pocket. 'One dollar, sir. An hour will be more than time enough.'

Wanglim took the dollar, bit it out of habit, and led the two men between rows of wooden pallets to a small room in the back. 'Tea?' he asked.

'Yes,' said Shoo Lee. 'Green.'

'Sir?' Wanglim said to Wilkinson.

'Tea? Yes, I suppose. Dark and thick, British style.'

'Have only Chinese style. No milk. No sugar,' Wanglim said.

'Whatever.' Wilkinson waved a hand in dismissal.

'Oolong,' Shoo Lee said. 'That should agree with Mr Wilkinson.'

'Good,' Wanglim said. He left.

'Now,' Shoo Lee indicated a low chair, 'please sit down. Let us discuss what brought you to Chinkburg, Mr Wilkinson.'

Wilkinson leaned forward and spoke in a low voice as if someone might be trying to overhear what he said. 'Listen, Shoo Lee. The A&P must get on with building the railroad.'

'Across Canyon Diablo?'

'No. It will take some months for engineers to survey the gorge, design a trestle for it, have the steel components made, and ship them out here to be assembled across the canyon.'

'Tea,' Wanglim said, then opened the door. He set one small porcelain cup of green tea before Shoo Lee and one of brown tea in front of Wilkinson. 'Call if you want more,' he said.

'He speaks English very well,' Wilkinson said.

'Most Chinese do,' said Shoo Lee.

He sipped from the teacup. 'But sometimes it's better if we appear witless before whitemen.'

'He even speaks English to you.'

'That's because I am not Chinese,' said Shoo Lee. 'Also, there are people here from Canton and Hong Kong. They speak Cantonese. And the people from Fukien and south China speak Fukienese. Those from Formosa speak Taiwanese. We speak English, which is the only language we all understand.'

Wilkinson nodded. 'Then you Orientals understand everything we say?'

'Most everything.'

'Interesting. I shall remember that.'

'Please. But about building more track.'

Wilkinson took a deep breath. 'Shoo Lee, you showed me that you know how to get a difficult job done on time and within budget.'

'Budget?'

'Yes. That means the agreed price. No more. No less.'

'What about building the railroad on the other side of Canyon Diablo?'

'Just that,' Wilkinson said. 'We can't hold up building the road just because of one trestle.'

'Rails are very heavy. How are they to get across?'

'That's part of the problem. But assume there are rails on the other side. Assume you don't have to worry about a supply of rails. How much track can you lay per day?'

Shoo Lee's face was placid as ever, but the fire in his eyes betrayed his interest. 'You want me to take charge of laying track for A&P?'

'In a word, yes.'

Still, at Wilkinson's confirmation, Shoo Lee's eyes widened and his jaw dropped. 'Me? Mr Wilkinson, I'm just a dumb Chink around here. Who's going to listen to a dumb Chink?'

'Anyone who wants a job building this railroad is going to have to listen to you, Shoo Lee. That'll be the only way they can get work.'

Inside, Shoo Lee grimaced. 'White-man bosses make lots of money from the railroad,' he said. 'They will be very angry.'

'Let them boil. They've cost the A&P an extravagant sum to get this far. We'd like to pare expenses down to a more normal level. You can do that, I wager.'

'I'm not anxious to be dead,' Shoo Lee said.

'We can protect you,' Wilkinson said.

Shoo Lee snorted. 'Mr Wilkinson. This is Diablo. Only the very strongest or the invisible survive here. It has nothing to do with law.'

'You survive.'

'Yes. By being like sparrows. Little birds that no one feels are dangerous. With your proposal, Mr Wilkinson, we will become very dangerous to many, and all will be able to see us.'

Wilkinson cut to the chase. 'Will you do it?'

Shoo Lee knew he might not come out alive. But he felt it was important to show that a man with colored skin could manage and accomplish a complex job as well as any white man.

'Yes,' he said. 'But you must wait until after I fight Butch Kennedy.'

* * *

Shawn Brodie rode through the night with two dead men bringing up the rear. As the dawn clawed at the eastern horizon he came upon Guy Rankin sitting his buckskin like he was waiting for someone. He watched from under the brim of his Stetson as Shawn got closer.

'Damn.'

'They shot at me, boss. All I could do was use your Winchester to even up the score.'

'Two of them, one of you?'

'Actually there were three of them.'

'Where's the other one?'

'Just a boy, boss. And not a very smart one at that. I don't think he'll be stealing Lazy EP cows ever again. These two won't either.'

Rankin didn't say a word. He just looked at the bodies hanging limp over their own saddles. He took a deep breath. 'Ain't never killed nobody myself,' he said.

'Hadn't we oughta take 'em back to the ranch in case someone there knows who they are? Might be good to let guys who might think of rustling Lazy EP cows know what happens to that kind of rannie.'

'Yeah. I reckon. The cows and calves is back on the range. Let's just beeline for the ranch,' Rankin said. He turned the buckskin and lined out like he didn't want to be too close to those dead men. Shawn followed, leading the rustlers' horses. It still took them most of the day to reach the Lazy EP headquarters.

A buggy stood in the front yard. The moment he saw it, Guy Rankin heeled his buckskin into a gallop. The best Shawn could get out of the rustlers' horses was a stiff-legged trot. He pulled

Pocoueno up near the buggy a good quarter of an hour after Rankin disappeared into the front door.

A heavy man burst from the door as Shawn slowed Pocoueno to a walk. Rankin came out of the house as if he were the man's shadow.

'Brodie,' he hollered. 'This here's Mr Peel.'

So this is the man who owes Tin Can Evans $3,000, then. Shawn lifted his battered Stetson.

'Pleased to meet you, sir,' he said. Mrs. Strickland, the warden's wife, had taught him manners.

'Brodie, you say?'

'Yes, sir. Shawn Brodie.'

'Rankin says you got the rustlers.'

'They shot at me, sir. I had no choice.'

Peel rubbed his hands together. 'You did right, young man. You did right.'

He walked around Pocoueno to the two horses with dead men in their saddles. 'Damn the rustlers. Damn them.'

Peel grabbed a handful of hair and lifted a head so he could see the bloated face. 'Don't know him.' He lifted the other one's head. 'Him neither.'

'If none of the riders know 'em, we'll just plant them,' Rankin said.

'Yeah. That's all we can do, I reckon.' Peel looked up at Shawn. 'You wanna come on into the house, boy?'

Shawn stiffened. 'Not meaning to talk back to you, Mr Peel, but it takes more than some passing boy to bring back two of the men who rustle Lazy EP cows belly down over their own saddles. I may not drink nothing harder than Arbuckles, but that's my choice. And when I pull a trigger, sir, the bullet goes where I aim it.' He sat square in Pocoueno's saddle and waited to see what Peel would do.

The Lazy EP owner stopped short, his head down like he might be looking at his toes. Then he raised his head and turned to face Shawn.

'Son, I had no intention of belittling you by calling you boy. From where I stand, you're young enough to be my own son. And I've gotta agree. No passing boy's gonna bring me two rustlers belly down over their own saddles. You done good, Shawn, and I'd appreciate it if you'd step into the house.'

Shawn nodded and climbed down off Pocoueno. He left the reins dragging the ground because he knew the tall horse would stand as still as if he'd been tied to a post. He used his hat to slap dust off his trousers, then put it back on his head and followed Peel and Rankin into the house.

'Gabby,' Peel hollered. 'Coffee for three.'

A large oval table with eight chairs around it dominated the room. Shawn wondered if Peel had a family. He'd seen no evidence of any. Bachelor? Or family living somewhere else — Flagstaff, Prescott, San Francisco? Peel hung his own hat on a tree by the door. Rankin and Shawn did the same. Peel sat in the chair furthest from the front door. He waved a hand at chairs on each side of the table. 'You boys can sit there,' he said. Rankin didn't seem to mind being called a boy, so Shawn didn't mention it again. They took their seats.

'Shawn Brodie. That is your name, right?'

'Yes, sir.'

'I don't remember you belonging to the Lazy EP crew.'

'No, sir. Rankin, er, the foreman said I could ride for a dollar a day and found, but that you'd have to give your approval for it to be a regular job.'

'Do you want to ride for the Lazy EP? Do you plan to stick around long enough to make it worth my while to hire you?'

'Yes, sir. I can ride and I can rope a bit. My gun shoots where I aim it, and I can do OK in a knock-down-drag-out. I reckon I can earn my keep and learn stuff from Rankin and the other hands at the same time.'

Peel laughed. 'Now that was a real speech.'

'Coffee, boss,' Gabby said, hustling into the room with his gnarled fingers hooked through the handles of three stoneware mugs. 'Fresh-brewed and strong enough to stand a spoon up in.' He put a mug in front of each man, and left as if he had better things to do in the kitchen.

Peel sipped at the brew. Shawn and Rankin followed suit.

'Damn,' Peel said. 'I spend half my time in Diablo or Flagstaff or Prescott and I can't find one place that makes coffee as good as Gabby. Reckon I'll have to raise his pay.'

'Don't let him hear you say that, boss,' Rankin said. 'His head's big enough already.'

'It's good,' Shawn said.

'You said something about knock-down-drag-out fighting, Shawn,' Peel said. 'There's gonna be one in Diablo on Friday. Butch Kennedy's gonna beat the shit outta some little Chink. Should be fun to watch. Maybe we oughta give the boys the day off.

Celebrate catching those rustlers.'

'Do you know who the Chink is, sir?' Shawn asked.

Peel looked at the ceiling. 'What the hell did they say he was? I never can remember Chink names. Wait. Choo-choo? Nah. Shoo. Shoo something or other.'

'Was it Shoo Lee?'

Peel gave Shawn a sharp look. 'Yeah. That's it. How'd you know?'

Shawn didn't answer, directly. 'Mr Peel. Would you be offended if I gave you a tip?'

Peel set his coffee cup back on the table. 'A tip? What kind of tip?'

'One that could make you a lot of money, maybe.'

'Shoot.'

'Mr Peel. I know Shoo Lee personal. He was my cellmate at Yuma Prison. And he can beat the shit out of any white man alive. If I were you, sir, I'd put my money on Shoo Lee. I ain't got much, but that's what I plan to do.'

'You was in Yuma?'

'I was.'

'What for?'

'Some people accused me of stealing a cow. It weren't true, but who'll believe a fourteen-year-old boy? I got pardoned.'

'You knew the Chink in there?'

'Shoo Lee ain't a Chink. He's from a place called Okinawa. And he knows how to fight like you'd never believe. No one in Yuma ever messed with Shoo Lee. Not even the guards. A big old guard sergeant went to hit Shoo Lee with a baton one day and in the blink of an eye Shoo Lee had the baton in his own hand. He handed it back, and told the sergeant that he'd do what the sergeant ordered, but he'd never allow the sergeant or a guard to strike him with a baton. They never did.'

'Sheesh.'

'I know I ain't got the right to say so, Mr Peel, but if you're a betting man, put your money on Shoo Lee.' He paused. 'I'd like to go to the fight, too,

130

sir. If it's OK. If we're getting a day off.'

Peel downed his coffee. 'Hell's a fire. Why not? Day after tomorrow, everybody gets a day off.'

8

Samuel Jones liked the crowds that betting on the coming Kennedy-Lee bout brought to the Poker Flat. Some always stayed. And some of those sat at his table, and left some of their sometimes-earned cash behind when they left. Said cash went straight into Samuel's pockets and helped pay his $1,000-a-month table rent.

Keno Harry had pasted betting odds on the mirror behind the bar. Two to one for bets on Butch Kennedy to win. Not much, but still, double the money put down if Butch won. And everyone expected him to win. After all, his opponent was a Chink. A man much smaller than Butch, probably about half Butch's hefty weight. Of course Butch would win.

Some people, however, liked to bet on the long shot. And betting on Shoo

Lee the Chinaman to beat Butch defined the long shot. Seven to one. Bet a dollar, get seven dollars from Keno Harry if the Chinaman wins.

These days the denizens of Diablo liked to play poker. Five-card stud was the norm. At the moment, four players and Samuel sat at his six-seat table. He'd just dealt five cards to each player and himself when he glanced at the mirror behind the bar, as was his habit now. Ellison Peel, his cowboys, and Gabby the cook pushed into the Poker Flat and strode to the bar.

Samuel could barely hear what Peel said over the rumble of the crowd in the Poker Flat.

'Who's taking the bets for the fight tomorrow?'

Keno Harry ducked inside the bar. 'I'm holding the bets,' he said.

The cowboys formed a half-circle about Peel. 'Me and my boys would like to place bets,' Peel said.

'Put your money on the bar,' Keno Harry said.

'You got it,' Peel said. He plonked a poke on the bar. 'There's fifty double eagles,' he said. 'I bet on the Chinaman to win.'

Samuel couldn't hear what Peel said, but the murmur of the gamblers in the Poker Flat soon told him.

'Peel's bet a thousand on the Chinaman.'

'No shit! A thousand? What the hell does he know?'

'Damned if I know, how the hell *should* I know?'

'A thousand.'

Keno Harry's face showed nothing. He was, after all, a gambler. 'One thousand on the Chinaman at odds of seven to one.' He took the poke, scribbled on a piece of paper, and handed the paper to Peel.

'Have at it, boys,' Peel said.

'Thirty bucks on the Chinaman,' said the first cowboy. Samuel recognized him as Guy Rankin, Peel's foreman.

The other Peel cowboys bet the same amount, except one.

'How about you?' Keno Harry said to the young blond man.

'Yes, thank you,' he said. 'May I bet one hundred dollars on Shoo Lee, please?' He placed five double eagles on the bar. 'At seven to one.'

Keno Harry wrote out a receipt for the money. 'Glad to take your money, cowboy, but hadn't you ought to bet some on Kennedy, too? Balance the scales, so to say?'

The blond cowboy smiled. 'Shoo Lee will win,' he said, and tucked the receipt into the pocket of his loose-fitting cotton shirt. As he stepped away from the bar, Samuel noticed he didn't wear boots. Well-worn moccasins encased the man's feet.

Samuel crooked his finger at Maisie. She ambled over with a drink in her hand, the same drink she'd been holding for nearly two hours now.

'Maisie gal, see that young blond man with Peel's cowboys? Could you ask him to come over here?'

'Pleasure,' she said, and walked away,

hips swinging. She wormed her way through the drinkers and gamblers to the blond cowboy's side. She spoke to him and motioned at Samuel's table. The blond youngster nodded and made his way to Samuel's table.

'Samuel Jones?'

Samuel stood up. 'Excuse me for a moment, gentlemen,' he said to the four men at the table. He stuck his hand out to the young cowboy. 'Yes, Samuel Jones. Pleased to make your acquaintance.'

'Shawn Brodie. Shark Blanchard told me about you. Said you were straight, awful good, but straight.'

Samuel raised an eyebrow. 'Shark? I've not seen him for some years. He dealt cards in Wolf Creek at the Eldorado, a much more upscale establishment than the Lucky Break, where I worked.'

'Shark's good. Taught me all I know about the pasteboards.'

'Would you like to sit in?'

Brodie grinned. 'You want me sitting

in? Me? I learned from Shark.'

Samuel turned to the men at the table. 'Gentlemen. Do you have any objection to Mr Brodie joining our friendly game?'

'None at all,' said a man in a single-button suit and short-brimmed hat. 'More the merrier, they say.'

The others nodded and raised their hands in greeting.

Samuel introduced them. 'Mr Smithson, a drummer waiting for the stage to Flagstaff and on to Prescott. Mr Heath, who tends the station building for A&P. And Mr Gregory, who has been somewhat vague about what he does.'

'Obliged,' Brodie said. 'Ride for the Lazy EP.' He took the single empty chair at Samuel's table. 'What's the game?' he asked.

'Five-card stud,' Samuel said. 'Just a few minutes while we finish this hand, if you please.'

'Sure.' Brodie sat and watched while the others continued their game.

Samuel watched Brodie with eyes

that had seen and measured hundreds of men. He didn't look at Brodie directly, but kept him within his peripheral vision. The young man sat as still as death. The excited cries of winners and the groans of losers may have registered on his hearing, but he didn't show it. Rather, his eyes picked a spot in the mid-distance and remained focused on that spot while Samuel and his opponents played the game. He seemed to be looking at nothing, yet seeing everything. *Strange youngster. Very strange.*

A ruckus arose at the roulette table.

'Sure, and ya may carry a big shillelagh in this town, Peel, but here's the Poker Flat where any boyo with a dime can have a go. So step back with ye and take your own turn when your own turn comes, I say.'

Pitch the guard snapped his 10-gauge closed and started to get down off his high seat, but Shawn Brodie's reaction was quicker. He inserted himself between Peel and the angry Irishman who'd yelled at him.

'I ride for the Lazy EP, mister. I'll not have you coming down on him like that. If you want to rail, try railing on me.'

'Ya little pipsqueak, you are. I'm half a mind to kick yer britches into next week, I am.'

Brodie smiled, but it was not a nice smile to see. 'Mister, you couldn't kick your way out of a ladies' sewing circle, so don't go telling me what you think you can do to me. Because you can't.'

'It's OK, Brodie. Leave it be,' Peel said.

'Can't have a mick talking down to you, Mr Peel. People need to respect you,' Brodie said.

Two more Irishmen joined the first. 'Well, boyo. Are ready to take on all of Eire, then? Come to think on it, won't take all, just three stalwarts from County Cork.' One kicked a chair out of the way so he'd have a clear swing at Brodie, if things got that far.

Brodie laughed. He stood five-ten or

so, and looked as slim as a willow tree. 'Three of you are not enough, men of Ireland. Not nearly enough.'

'We'll not have any slug outs in here,' Pitch Duggan said. 'Keno Harry don't allow it.' He shoved the heavy shotgun between the Irishmen and Brodie.

'Bloody hell. You got what it takes out on Hell Street, boyo? You don't and I'll push your precious boss man's nose in the nearest pile of horse shit, I will.'

Brodie bowed extravagantly from the waist and waved his hand toward the door.

After you, gentle . . . micks. Hell Street or wherever in hell you prefer. Excuse me, Mr Peel. These men must be put in their places.'

The Irishmen shoved their way through the crowd that had gathered around, removing their shirts as they went. One palmed a bar of lead for his right hand.

Customers of Poker Flat poured out of the door with the three Irishmen.

Shawn didn't feel as confident as he

might have looked. But he had to make an even stronger impression on Ellison Peel if his plan to recover Tin Can Evans's $3,000 was to work out.

Outside the Poker Flat he also stripped off his shirt. By now, the Lazy EP riders were behind him, buffering him from the crowd. He handed the shirt to Guy Rankin.

'Boss, look after that, please. And this.' He handed Rankin a billfold and a poke. 'It's all I've got in the world.'

He stepped out of his moccasins and left them on the porch. The Irishmen were a formidable line in front of him. Three big men with muscles that bulged from their manual labor and with bellies that bulged from the beer they quaffed. They pulled suspenders up over their union suits and stood shoulder to shoulder. He'd have to separate them if he were to have any hope of winning.

'Eamon Cooney. Don't you think three against one is a bit over-matched?' Samuel Jones spoke from just outside the door of the Poker Flat. '"Twould seem to me that one at a time might be more manly, if you are bound and determined to fight this lad.'

'Thank you, Mr Jones, but they're the ones who called me out,' Shawn said. He went three steps toward the Irishmen. Two stepped back and let Cooney lead. Their faces said they were certain the big man would put the skinny kid in his place. Cooney put up his fists in imitation of a prizefighter. Shawn smiled.

Cooney took a long step forward and swung a ponderous roundhouse at Shawn's jaw. Shawn moved only a fraction, but enough that the fist whizzed by and Cooney staggered a step to the right.

'Yah,' Shawn said and drove a hard fist into Cooney's unprotected kidney. He continued the move and caught Cooney behind the knee with a sweeping kick. The Irishman sprawled, his face twisted in pain. Shawn stood back, his knees slightly bent and his fists at the tops of his thighs. He watched Cooney, but could see the other two in his peripheral vision.

'Up, laddie,' one shouted. 'He's just waiting there for ye.'

Cooney gingerly got to his feet. Again he faced Shawn, but this time without the assurance he showed before. He shuffled toward the slim bare-footed cowboy, who was now without his hat. Then he lunged, his arms out to capture Shawn in a fierce bear hug.

Again Shawn stepped lightly aside. Cooney stumbled. The Lazy EP cowboys turned him around and shoved him back towards the center of the ring formed by onlookers.

Cooney's two friends looked undecided.

'Come on, Cooney. Come on. You were going to give me a licking, weren't you?' Shawn stood with his feet shoulder-width apart, one slightly ahead of the other. His right fist was curled and tucked close to his ribs.

The other was straight out at a forty-five-degree angle.

'Arrrgh.' Cooney charged again.

This time, Shawn stepped in to meet his charge, stabbing out with his right hand and striking Cooney in the breastbone, first and second knuckles flat against the Irishman's chest. The impact sounded as if a sledgehammer had hit Cooney. Almost as quickly as he struck, Shawn withdrew the fist and smashed the heel of his left hand against Cooney's chin. The force thrust the Irishman's jawbone against his carotid arteries long enough to rob him of consciousness. He toppled to the street and lay still.

Shawn turned toward the other two Irishmen. 'One at a time or two at once, don't make no matter. You micks ain't gonna fool with my boss, got that?'

'You sumbitchin' kid. Gitchurself ready for a beating.' Both men rushed at Shawn, only to find him not there. He had spun away, lifting a leg in a classic kara ti move and slammed the horn-hard edge of his foot into the nearest man's neck. The move continued on as the man dropped to his knees, holding his throat and choking. The foot that Shawn kicked with before now became his pivot leg, and his other leg scribed an arc toward the other Irishman. His foot smashed into the Irishman's jaw, and Shawn spun around, planting his feet and readying his iron-hard fists. He surveyed the ring.

Cooney was out. Another Irishman was on his hands and knees, still coughing from Shawn's foot to the throat. The third man lay out, his face lopsided. He breathed, but who knew for how long.

'I think the fight's over,' Shawn said. He reached for his shirt and valuables.

Rankin handed them over. 'I ain't never seen nothing like that,' he said, awe in his voice.

'Man picks up strange skills in a place like Yuma prison,' Shawn said. 'Sorry to disturb things for you, Mr

Peel,' he added. He picked up his hat from the porch, set it on his head and reached for his moccasins.

'Why don't you get a decent pair of boots, kid?' Rankin said.

'Don't want my feet to get soft,' Shawn said. He stepped closer to Rankin and said in a low voice. 'Shoo Lee taught me to fight when I was in prison with him. Only he's a helluvalot better than me.'

'Sheesh.'

'Yeah.'

'Lazy EP,' Peel called. 'Beer's on me.'

A cheer rose from the Lazy EP cowboys, and they rushed into the Poker Flat to test its brew.

Peel waited for Shawn. 'Where'd you ever learned to fight like that?' he asked.

Shawn grinned and ducked his head. 'Man learns a lot in the Hell Hole,' he said, 'else he dies.'

'Good job you did.' Peel patted Shawn on the arm. 'Have a drink on me?'

'Sure, Mr Peel. I ride for the brand, and that's the Lazy EP. A beer would taste right good.' Shawn turned his back on Hell Street and took two steps toward the door of the Poker Flat. Ellison Peel moved in behind Shawn just as a shot sounded from the street.

'Umph,' Peel said and slumped forward. He clutched at Shawn and crumpled to the porch, bleeding.

'Lazy EP,' Shawn shouted. 'Lazy EP. Man down. Man down.'

A man in the street leveled his revolver for a second shot, but Shawn Brodie had already flung a sharp piece of metal shaped like a four-pronged spur rowel. The rowel-like weapon struck the gunman in the forehead and sank two inches through his skull and into his brain. He fell on his face, pulling the trigger of his pistol as he went down. The bullet ricocheted from the stones of Hell Street and smashed into one of the porch poles of the Poker Flat.

Guy Rankin leaped over Ellison

Peel's crumpled form, six-gun in hand. He knelt in front of his brand's owner, facing the street. Four other cowboys and Gabby the cook pushed their way through the door as well, and half a dozen cocked revolvers covered the men in the street.

'You all want a shootout,' Rankin hollered, 'open the ball. Lazy EP riders'll leave you lying in your own blood, by all that's holy I swear it.'

The crowd faded away, leaving the senseless Cooney and his associates lying in the street. Someone grabbed the dead shooter and dragged him off. No doubt denizens of Diablo would have him stripped and discarded before his body was cool.

'Rankin,' Shawn said, 'the boss's hit bad. If he don't get a real doc, we may lose him. Says he can't feel nothing.'

Samuel Jones spoke up from his position beside the door. 'The train to Winslow should be pulling out in less than an hour. Might be a good idea to get Peel on it. I hear there's a good doc by the name of Kinderly, Malcom Kinderly, in Winslow. Worth a try.'

The Lazy EP riders found an old door to act as a stretcher for their fallen boss, and carried him to the stone station building at the edge of Canyon Diablo. The engine had steam built up and was ready to pull out as soon as Ronald Wilkinson returned from wherever he had gone.

'Hey,' Rankin hailed the engineer. 'Gunshot man here. Need to get him to Winslow to see Doc Kinderly.'

Gabby had worked with bandannas from the cowboys to stanch Peel's bleeding. The ranch owner himself was conscious but groggy, still complaining about being unable to feel his hands or feet.

'Don't you worry, boss,' Rankin said. 'We'll get you to the doc in Winslow.'

'Rankin,' Peel whispered. 'Rankin, you . . . you take . . . take the riders back to the ranch. Keep it up. Don't let nobody . . . nobody tear it down. Watch the cows . . . ride with rifles ready. Hear?'

'Who's gonna watch you?' Rankin asked.

Peel cleared his throat. 'Umm. Brodie . . . Brodie 'n' Gabby. You all watch . . . the ranch. Go.'

'What is this? What's going on?' Ronald Wilkinson strode up to the group of cowboys on the station platform.

'Mr Wilkinson?' Rankin asked.

'That's right. So what?'

'I'm Guy Rankin, *Segundo* over at the Lazy EP. Our boss's been shot. Need to get him to Winslow so Doc Kinderly can take care of him. Need to put him on your train, Mr Wilkinson, with your permission, of course.' Rankin stood with his hat in his hand.

'Of course. Put him in my car, the caboose. There's a bottle of laudanum in the medicine cabinet if he gets to hurting too much. Who's going with him?'

'Me,' Shawn Brodie said. 'Me and Gabby here.'

'Fine. Get the man aboard.'

Less than five minutes later the A&P train to Winslow pulled out, with Shawn Brodie and Gabby watching over Ellison Peel as he lay on Wilkinson's own bunk.

9

The hour and ten minutes to Winslow felt like half a century to Shawn. He and Gabby hovered over Ellison Peel like mother hens. The rancher lay still, except when the motion of the caboose jostled him, and when he moved, he groaned, as if by reaction. Other than that, he seemed dead.

'How's he doing?' Wilkinson asked from the rear door of the caboose.

'Breathing, sir,' Shawn said. 'Can't tell much more than that.'

'Pulling in directly. I had the station attendant in Diablo wire ahead. Someone should be waiting to take Mr Peel to Doc Kinderly's place.'

'Thanks, Mr Wilkinson. Could be our boss owes you his life.'

'Let's hope so. He's a lucky man to have men like you working for him.'

The train's whistle blasted and the

train slowed, chuffing and puffing as the engineer applied the brakes. The moment it came to a stop someone jumped on to the caboose's rear platform and pounded on the door.

Wilkinson opened it.

'Wounded man, you say?' The pounder carried a leather bag. 'I'm Kinderly. Let me see that man.'

'Over here, Doc,' Shawn said, pulling aside the curtains that had kept Peel's bunk private. 'This is Ellison Peel, owner of the Lazy EP ranch over by Diablo Canyon.'

Kinderly quickly examined Peel. 'Well done. Stopping the bleeding like that means a lot. We'll take him to my clinic and go from there. Let me get some help.'

'We can carry him,' Shawn said. 'Me and Gabby. You got a stretcher? Or do we use the door?'

'Time is of the essence, young man. Use the door.'

Gabby and Shawn positioned the door and gently moved Peel on to it.

The wounded man groaned, and Shawn grimaced.

'Reaction, young man. He's reacting to being moved. Shows he's still fighting. Carry on.'

Gabby took the foot end and Shawn carried the end under Peel's head and shoulders. When they got through the door at the back of the caboose two railroad men helped them lift the door with Peel on it over to the platform and on to a light buckboard pulled by matched bay geldings. Doctor Kinderly picked up the reins and clucked to the team. They walked sedately down the street and around the corner with the doctor alongside. He pulled the buckboard up in front of a frame house with a shingle that read Malcom Kinderly MD.

'Help bring him in,' Kimberly said.

Shawn and Gabby once again picked up the door and carried Ellision Peel into Doc Kinderly's clinic.

'On the examination table, gentlemen,' Kinderly said. 'Let's get a good look at him. Face down, if you please.'

Again, Peel groaned as the cowboys moved him. Shawn and Gabby stood back as Doctor Kinderly went to work.

'This bandage was well done,' Kimberly said as he removed the temporary bandage from Peel's wound. 'Hmmm. Slanting. Mr Peel? Do you hear me, Mr Peel?'

'I hear you.' Peel's voice was weak, a shadow of his normal powerful one.

'Does the wound pain you much, Mr Peel?' Kinderly asked.

'Can't feel much of anything. No fingers. No toes. No nothing.'

'We'll have a look then,' Kinderly said. He washed his hands with some kind of solution from a bottle, then probed at the wound. Peel said nothing.

'Bullet hit the spine and changed direction. It's sitting on your ribs not an inch under the skin. It'll only take a minute to cut it out,' the doctor said.

'Can't feel anything, Doc. Feet, legs, hands, arms, nothing.'

'As I said, the bullet hit your spine,

155

Mr Peel. That's what's causing your inability to feel your extremities. I've read about cases similar to yours, and I predict that you will begin to regain feeling within days. No more than a week or maybe two. Now, let me get that bullet out.'

As Kinderly had said, the simple operation took minutes, and required only a stitch to close up the incision. His skilled hands cleaned and sutured the entry wound as well, and he used adhesive plasters to cover clean gauze pads over the wounds.

'Fine. Very fine. Now,' he said, turning to Shawn and Gabby. 'I think Mr Peel should stay here for a few days. I'd like to keep him under observation to see how quickly he regains the feeling in his extremities.'

'Maybe we oughta stick around,' Shawn said. 'Maybe help out or something. Maybe . . . '

Doc Kinderly chuckled. 'Nothing to worry about at the moment, young man. Mr Peel's life is in no danger. And

I feel rather certain he'll start regaining sensation in his limbs soon. No need for both of you to stay. One would be a help, however.'

'Gabby, can you stay with the boss? I've got an errand to run here in Winslow, then I need to get back to Diablo before Shoo Lee fights,' Shawn said.

'Sure enuff,' Gabby said. 'Leave it to me. You pick up my winnings, will ya?'

Shawn laughed. 'May be a lot o' people pissed off after the fight. I'll watch my step, I reckon.' He shook hands with the doctor. 'Take care of our boss,' he said. 'He's a good man.'

'Not to worry, young man. He'll be up and around within the week, I'd wager.'

Leaving Doc Kinderly's place, Shawn replaced his short-brimmed hat. He still wore the moccasins he'd put on to fight the Irishmen so it was easy to walk the six blocks to Tin Can Evans's lair.

One of Tin Can's bodyguards blocked the door.

'Need to see Tin Can,' Shawn said.

'Says who?'

'Shawn Brodie.'

The strongarm hollered over his shoulder. 'Some asshole here to see Tin Can. Says he's Shawn Brodie. Know him?'

Another gorilla came from inside the house. 'Let 'im in.'

The strongarm stepped aside. 'Little shitass like you. I oughta wipe the sidewalk with your pretty face before I let you in.'

Shawn gave him a little grin. Then walked past him into the dark inner sanctum of Tin Can Evans.

'Brodie, Brodie. When ya gonna grow up? Good to see you, though.' Tin Can's voice came as if from a dark dungeon.

'You smoking hash back there, Tin Can?'

'Nah. Just tobacco. Burley. Kinda sweet-smelling, don'cha think?'

Shawn wrinkled his nose. 'Don't like the stuff,' he said. 'Just the smell's enough to kill a man.'

'Didn't expect you back so soon.'

'Boss's at Doc Kinderly's place. Got shot in the back up to Diablo. Brung him down on the A&P. Be all right the doc says.'

'Boss?'

'Yeah,' Shawn said. 'I ride for the Lazy EP.'

'No shit.'

'Tin Can. Ellison Peel's a good man. I ain't talked to him about his debt, but I reckon he's got a good reason for not paying up yet.'

'Good men still get too far in debt. He owes me.'

'You'll get your money back, Tin Can. I'm saying it. And I don't lie. I just gotta have a little time.'

'That's what they all say, kid. Ever' one who zilches on a debt starts off saying he needs a little time.' Tin Can's voice sounded hollow, coming from far back in his cave-like room.

'You lied to me, Tin Can, and you tried to cheat me. Lucky I caught you or you'd've squashed me like a bug. But when I tell you something, you can believe it ain't no lie. If you don't believe me, you can just take me off the job and let one of those hunks of lard outside do it for you.'

'Now, now. No cause to get upset. Take all the time you need. Like to next week or something.'

Shawn turned to leave. 'If one of your fat bouncers lays a hand on me, Tin Can, I swear, I'll beat him within an inch of his life, and don't you believe for a minute that I can't.'

'Steve,' Tin Can hollered.

'Whaddaya need, Mr Evans?'

'Shawn Brodie's leaving. Let him go in peace.'

The broad man called Steve laughed. 'I oughta teach him some manners, is what I oughta do,' he said.

Shawn gave Tin Can a long look. 'You OK, Tin Can? These guys don't sound like they respect you.'

'Never you mind,' Tin Can said. 'Just get your own job done.'

Shawn stood very still for a long minute. 'All right,' he said. 'I'm leaving.'

The two big men paid to make sure Tin Can Evans was cared for and safe stood side by side on the porch. They didn't block the way entirely, but Shawn had to detour around them to take the three steps down to the street.

'I'll be back,' he said, and struck out for the railway station.

Shawn walked from Tin Can Evans's lair to the A&P station. He knew he had plenty of time to board the train to Diablo. What he didn't know was that every footloose man in town, and more than a few women were crowding the platform, haggling for a ride.

'Your boss OK?' Ronald Wilkinson asked as Shawn climbed up on to the caboose platform.

'Man'd figure Diablo was a place to get out of, not get into,' Shawn said. 'Yeah, boss'll be fine, Doc Kinderly says. A week or so. Why the crowd?'

'Word of the Irish-Chink fight got

out. Everyone wants to get in on the betting and win some money. A grubstake, maybe.'

'Problem is, they think Kennedy's going to win.'

'I'd imagine so. Did you bet, Mr Brodie?'

Shawn gave Wilkinson an open grin. 'I surmise. I surely do. I just hope Keno Harry's straight and above board.'

A young man in a conductor's uniform called the traditional shout. 'Bo-o-o-oard. Alla Boooard!'

The engine puffed and chuttered, and the big drive wheels dug at the steel rails. Slowly the train moved away, gradually gaining speed as it headed toward Diablo. Shawn sat by a window and watched the land speed by, but his mind twiddled with images of town and the coming fight that would match his old cellmate with an Irishman twice his size.

★　★　★

Shoo Lee spent the early hours practicing his kara ti routines, doing heron poses and shark poses, and then running ten miles along the A&P tracks. One more day until the bout with Butch Kennedy. He was ready. But then he was ready every day. Those who were not ready did not live long in Diablo.

As he did his morning exercises he thought of the job Ronald Wilkinson wanted him to do. Wilkinson promised that A&P would get the rails and ties and spikes to the other side of Canyon Diablo. But the crews couldn't come back to Chinkburg every night. That meant food and shelter had to be set up over there. He decided to go to Flagstaff as soon as he beat Butch Kennedy. As soon as he could catch a ride. Freight wagons would take him, the stagecoach would not, even if he paid full fare.

Ten miles down the track and ten back. Shoo Lee's breathing was back to normal by the time he got to Ching

Wong's for breakfast — the only place where whites and blacks and yellows mixed without any problems. Of course, you just took your plate of food, ate it on the roadside, and pushed the plate back at Wong.

'Understand you know Shawn Brodie,' the cowman standing next to Shoo Lee said.

'Ummm,' Shoo Lee answered.

'I'm Guy Rankin,' the man said. '*Segundo* at the Lazy EP. Shawn's one of our riders. He's told us about you, and we're all putting our money on you to win the fight.'

Shoo Lee got his breakfast — a raw egg on a bowl of white steamed rice with soy sauce dribbled on it. He pulled a set of wooden chopsticks from his waistband, walked three steps down Hell Street, and began to mix egg and rice together. Rankin followed.

'Don't look like something I'd want to eat,' Rankin said. 'Not that I mind you eating it.'

Shoo Lee shoveled rice and egg and

sauce into his mouth over the side of the bowl, using the chopsticks to lever the mixture in. He chewed and swallowed.

'Rice gives me power,' he said. 'Egg helps build my body, so my ancestors say. The sauce just tastes good to me, a little salty.'

Rankin smiled. For the first time, an Oriental had spoken to him in straight English. 'You sound just like an American,' he said.

'A man loses his accent fast in Yuma,' Shoo Lee said. 'Shawn taught me some, too.'

'And you taught him.'

'Cellmates help each other survive.'

'He does good for a slim cowboy,' Rankin said, watching Shoo Lee scoop more rice and egg into his mouth.

Shoo Lee nodded, chewing slowly.

'So the fight's on at one in the afternoon, then?'

Shoo Lee nodded again, and finished the bowl of rice and egg. He handed the empty bowl back to Wong. 'I must go get myself ready.'

'Doing something special?'

Shoo Lee grinned. 'Maybe. Going to soak my hands and feet in mare's piss.' He laughed at Rankin's shocked look. 'Mare's piss toughens the skin,' he said. 'Pregnant mare is best, but any mare will do if no pregnant one is available.'

'Sheesh. Mare's piss.'

'Excuse me, I must make ready. Butch Kennedy will wait at one o'clock in front of Poker Flat.' Shoo Lee bowed to Rankin and walked swiftly down Hell Street to the crossing to Chinkburg. He was soon out of sight.

Rankin stood where he was for some minutes, thinking about a man soaking his hands and feet in mare's piss. He shook his head and made his way back to Poker Flat, where the rest of the Lazy EP cowboys sipped lukewarm beer.

★ ★ ★

Butch Kennedy was ready. Truly truly ready. *The bare-assed gall of that little Chink. Shit, he ain't even half my size. I'll wipe bloody Hell Street with his bloody face, that I will.*

Kennedy stood before the broad plank that served as a bar at the Road to Ruin. The saloon, only three doors down from Poker Flat, lacked even a smidgeon of its style. But the rotgut was potent and cheap. Working Irishmen went to Road to Ruin to drink. If they had any money extra, they went to Poker Flat to gamble. And if they worked a solid week, they'd celebrate at Clabberfoot Annie's once, then go to the cribs out back.

'Kin I buy you a drink, champ?' The man making the offer looked wall-eyed and his hands shook as he fingered in a worn leather wallet for money. 'Nope, guess I won't,' he said. 'Sorry.'

He stepped away, then stopped. 'Beat that filthy Oriental 'til he can't stand up, champ. Then I can buy you a drink, I can.'

Kennedy raised a hand. 'Look forward to it, Barbary,' he said. 'By all means.'

A gaggle of working men pushed through the door. 'Looking for Butch Kennedy,' one of them hollered.

'I'm here,' Kennedy said. 'What'll ye be wanting?'

'We're the Sons of Eire from Winslow, Mr Kennedy, come to give our compatriot some important moral support. We're here to watch you beat the livin' daylights outta that chinky cheek.' The man giggled. 'I mean cheeky Chink, that's what I mean.'

'Sons of Eire, are ye?'

'That we are, no doubt about it. And we put down a month's fair wages each on your winning of this crazy bout, we did. A full month's. The mister at Poker Flat, Keno Harry, he's called, he says the odds are less than two to one. So we'll not double our money, but still gain a nice bit of interest when you put the blimey Chink in his blimey place, we will.'

A battered clock clinging to a rickety wall by a single nail clanged the noon hour. 'Free lunch for ya, Butch?' the barkeep asked.

'I'll be fighting in an hour, Boyle. Maybe better not eat much. Just one long bun with a bit of salt pork and cheese.'

'Cheese? Your free lunch has cheese?' the Son of Eire asked. ' 'Twould be good to sink me pearlies into some cheese, it would.'

'Not free for nobody but the champ,' Boyle the barkeep said. 'Bread and pickles at the end of the bar. Help yerself. Drinks ain't free neither.'

The Sons of Eire scrambled for food. Moments later, Boyle brought Kennedy's sandwich along with a mug of beer. 'You whip that Chink, Butch. You do that.'

'I will,' Kennedy said. 'I surely will.' He took a huge bite of the bread, cheese, and meat. Chewing, he sucked at the beer. 'Damn good,' he said after he'd swallowed. He glanced down the bar at the Sons of Eire. They had made a big dent in the pile of bread, and each had a whiskey glass by his elbow. Kennedy grinned. Road to Ruin would make money this noontime, and when he cleaned the Chinaman's plow, he'd make a good bit of spending cash for himself, too. He couldn't help rubbing his hands together. Another big bite finished up the sandwich. Kennedy waved at the Winslow Sons of Eire. He walked out of the Road to Ruin, not even considering paying for his beer. A crowd gathered in front of Poker Flat, where two lariats and four railway spikes marked off a makeshift square. That was where the Chinaman would eat dirt. Kennedy wagged his shoulders and doubled up his fists. If ever there was a fight he was ready for, this was it.

10

Samuel Jones stood on the porch of Poker Flat, chewing at a twig he used to clean his teeth and scrutinizing the jostling rowdy crowd gathered around the fight ring.

'Isn't it exciting, Sam?' Maisie leaned over the porch rail with her hand over her brow. 'Do you really think the Chinaman will win?' she asked.

He removed the twig and spat over the rail. 'If he doesn't, we'll be out a pretty penny,' he said. 'But I read something in that man. He's fearless. Confident. Always ready.'

Half a dozen men barged out of Poker Flat. 'Where's Butch Kennedy?' one shouted. 'Just put thirty dollars on him winning. Wanna see how he's up for the fight. Butch! Butch!'

Butch Kennedy strode from the Road to Ruin, brushing crumbs from his mouth. 'I'm here, Willis, here.' He pulled a pocket watch from his vest by its chain. 'Five minutes yet until noon. Where's the Chink?'

Several in the crowd laughed. 'If he's smart, he won't show,' a man yelled.

Kennedy shed his jacket and vest. He rolled his sleeves up over massive forearms. He took a seat on the upended beer keg placed in the corner at the edge of Hell Street.

Jones shook his head. 'Damn Keno Harry's got me refereeing this fight,' he said. 'Hell of a lot I know about fist-fighting.'

'That's good,' Maisie said. 'If you are the referee, at least it will be fair.' She took a long look at Jones's face. The planes were hard and flat. Sharp lines ran from nostrils to the corners of his mouth. Crow's feet in the corners of his eyes. Slashes between his eyebrows. The easygoing Sam Jones of the bluff table was nowhere in sight. 'You will make it fair, right?' she asked.

'Hmmmm.' Jones's attention shifted

to the railroad track running down the south side of Hell Street behind the line of drinkeries and gambling places and dove roosts. A whistle sounded. Then came the chuffing of the A&P train as its drive wheels grabbed the rails and started the cars off toward Winslow. As it rumbled past, a flock of people came from Chinkburg. They came twenty people wide and fifteen or so deep. And at their head, bare to the waist and glittering with grease or something smeared all over his face and neck and torso, came Shoo Lee. He wore a pair of lightweight canvas trousers that came to midway between ankle and knee. They came silently. No cheers. No laughter. No catcalls. Just 300 Chinks and Mexes and Blacks. A crowd of 300 behind Shoo Lee.

Jones timed his stroll down the steps and along Hell Street so that he would reach the south edge of the fight ring about the same time as Shoo Lee.

'I'm to referee the fight, Shoo Lee, just to make sure all is fair and square.'

Shoo Lee stopped two paces short of the lariats on the ground.

'I am here,' he said. The Chinkburg residents who followed him fanned out in a semicircle behind him.

'You can sit there,' Jones said, indicating an overturned beer keg in the corner opposite Butch Kennedy. The Irishman showed his teeth in a snarl and bunched his fists as he stared at Shoo Lee, who calmly sat on the keg.

'I'm to referee this fight,' Samuel Jones said. He spoke loudly, but didn't holler. 'You all know me from Poker Flat. I always run a fair game. This fight will be the same. Now, Butch Kennedy, as the Oriental Shoo Lee is stripped to the waist, I'll expect you to do the same.'

'She-it,' Kennedy said, but he stripped off his shirt. 'Union suit's one piece,' he said. 'Cain't take it down.'

Jones took a slim knife from a little sheath in the small of his back. 'I'm going to ask you to cut the top off of it,' he said. 'I'll buy you a new union suit after the fight.'

'New one?'

Jones nodded. 'That's what I said.'

'Gimme the shiv.'

Jones handed the little knife to Kennedy.

'Bobby boyo, give me a hand, will ye not?' Kennedy gave the knife to another Irishman, who sliced the top off his union suit. 'That do, Jones?'

'It does.' Samuel Jones raised an eyebrow. 'And who is your second?'

'Ain't no duel,' Kennedy groused.

'Each man will have a second,' Jones said. 'This fight is a civilized one.'

'Then Bobby McGilly'll be mine, won'cha, Bobby boyo?'

'Aye,' said the Irishman with the knife.

Jones held out his hand for the knife, and McGilly handed it back. He slipped it into the sheath behind his belt as he turned toward Shoo Lee. 'And you, Mr Lee? Have you a second?'

'I'll be Shoo Lee's second.' The voice came from the porch of Poker Flat.

Jones looked over his shoulder, and

his eyebrow went up again. 'You, Mr Brodie?'

Shawn Brodie grinned. 'Glad I got back from Winslow in time, Samuel. You see, Shoo Lee was my bunkie at Yuma. I'll be his second.' He walked down Hell Street to stand behind his Okinawan friend.

'Mr Brodie seconds for Shoo Lee,' Samuel Jones intoned.

Shoo Lee sat on his beer keg as still as a statue. He'd shaved his head and perhaps his body, and greased his skin. He wore light cotton pants that hung to just below his knees. His broad feet were bare. Jones thought he looked strange, and then realized he'd shaved his eyebrows, too. The crowd rumbled.

'He's all yours, Butch,' a man yelled. 'Put the poxied Chink in his place. She-it, thinking he can fight a Irishman.'

'Yeah, yeah.' The crowd east and west of the ring, spread up and down Hell Street, bet on Butch Kennedy, bet on his broad shoulders and his bulging muscles, bet on his saloon-brawl reputation, and bet on white against yellow. 'Butch,' they hollered. 'Butch. Butch. Butch!'

Samuel Jones held his hands high in the air, signaling for silence. Butch glared across the ring at Shoo Lee, who examined the ground in front of him. But neither moved, except for the tic of a flexing muscle in the Irishman's torso.

'Ladies and gentlemen,' Jones said.

The crowd quieted a bit.

Jones lifted his voice. 'Ladies and gentlemen,' he repeated. 'Welcome. Welcome. Welcome to the greatest fight east of the Barbary Coast. In the west corner, we have Butch Kennedy, well known in Diablo for his skill in fisticuffs.'

The crowd roared. 'Butch. Butch. Butch.'

Jones held his hands up again. 'Please. Ladies and gentlemen. This is not a barroom brawl. It is a match of fisticuffs, west against east. Something we are not privileged to see every day.'

'Damn Chink,' someone yelled. The crowd rumbled again.

That is, the crowd lined up and down Hell Street rumbled. The one that had followed Shoo Lee across the A&P tracks from Chinkburg stood silent. They looked at Shoo Lee with something like hope in their eyes. Perhaps they'd put what little money they had on him to win.

'The rules, ladies and gentlemen. Any bout of fisticuffs must have rules. As this is a bare-knuckles contest, we shall adopt the London Prize Ring rules. As you see, the contestants are to fight within a square twenty-four feet to a side. If a fighter steps outside the square, his opponent shall move back to allow the fighter back inside the square. If a fighter is knocked down, the round ends. A one-minute rest period then ensues, but the knocked-down fighter must get to his feet within thirty seconds or forfeit the bout. Biting, headbutting, and punching below the belt are fouls, and if repeated after the referee's warning, the fighter who continually fouls will be declared loser.' Jones turned to Butch Kennedy.

'Mr Kennedy. Do you understand the rules?'

'What's not to understand?' Kennedy growled.

Jones shifted his gaze to Shoo Lee. 'Mr Lee. Do you understand the rules?'

'Yes, Mr Jones. I understand,' Shoo Lee said, his tone deferential.

'Well said, Mr Lee. May I ask what you have put on your face and torso?'

'Vaseline,' Shoo Lee said.

'Asshole,' Kennedy said.

Shoo Lee smiled with his lips but not his eyes. His shaved pate glistened. 'It's just petroleum jelly. That's all.'

'Not gonna help your ass,' Kennedy said. 'Not even a little bit.'

Shoo Lee's smile never left his lips. He bowed his head to Butch Kennedy.

'The contestants will stand,' Jones intoned.

The crowd seemed to hold its collective breath. Jones stepped to the edge of the square.

'Let the fight begin!'

Kennedy jumped to his feet and strode across the square, his fists doubled up but swinging at his side. The big Irishman stood slightly over six feet and looked like a collection of beer barrels with his stumpy legs. No one doubted his power. Still, a rather thick layer of fat encircled his midriff and it jiggled as he walked.

Shoo Lee took two long steps toward the center of the fighting square and stopped, one foot slightly ahead of the other with his knees slightly bent. His left fist rested fingers up at his waist. His right arm was elbow-locked into a solid immovable stavelike position with a fist at its end. He waited for Kennedy to attack.

Samuel Jones angled around to where he could see both fighters. He watched closely. No one cheated at his poker table, none would cheat in this fight. That's how Samuel Jones operated.

Butch Kennedy hunched, rounding his shoulders and keeping his elbows to his sides. He'd been in too many saloon brawls to open himself up. His hamlike fists made circles in the air.

Shoo Lee didn't move. He lowered his head and watched Kennedy from beneath his shaved brow. He didn't move, but somehow exuded the tension of a coiled spring.

'Come on, asshole Chink,' Kennedy growled. 'This here's a gawldam fight, not a stand-off.'

'I am here,' Shoo Lee said. 'I will stay here.'

'Then I'll just hafta knock you on your cracker ass.' Kennedy shuffled closer and bunched his shoulders, preparing for a roundhouse swing that would knock the Chinaman clean out of the ring. He towered over Shoo Lee but somehow didn't look overpowering compared to the Oriental. The last two steps were swift and straight. Kennedy's right shoulder moved back as he readied his smashing swing. For an instant, his left shoulder pointed at Shoo Lee and his torso tensed for the roundhouse.

Kennedy swung . . .

The instant Kennedy moved Shoo Lee moved as well. He moved slightly, but enough for Kennedy's ponderous fist to whistle by as he turned his face away. The momentum of the would-be blow carried Kennedy by Shoo Lee, who shifted his weight and sent two swift, lightning-like blows into Kennedy's right kidney. The Irishman staggered and nearly went to one knee.

'Butch. Butch. Butch.' The crowd roared, but the sound did not bear the easy confidence of a bare minute ago. 'Smash 'im down. Stomp 'im. Beat 'im to a pulp.' Different voices shouting the same thing.

Shoo Lee once again took the same place and stance he'd held when Kennedy tried the roundhouse.

Kennedy squared his shoulders. 'Gonna take you, Chinaman. Purely gonna take you.'

Shoo Lee shifted to face Kennedy straight on.

As Kennedy got close he threw a straight punch aimed at Shoo Lee's face. Shoo Lee moved slightly and used his iron-hard left forearm to block the Irishman's blow and turn it aside. Before Kennedy could recover, Shoo Lee's right fist, elbow locked with the full weight of his upper body behind it, smashed into his sternum like a hammer splatting against a side of beef.

In reaction, Kennedy's arms wrapped around Shoo Lee, but he merely ducked away, and the arms slipped off the layer of Vaseline covering Shoo Lee's head and upper body. His lips curved upward slightly as he stepped away and once more took his defiant stance.

Kennedy shook his head, then lowered it like a bull.

'You stinky slick little Chinaman, you. You'll not make a fool of Darren Kennedy, you surely won't.' He took two steps to close the distance to Shoo

Lee. Fists closed, forearms up to block Shoo Lee's blows, Kennedy readied himself again. But this time, while drawing his right arm back as if to strike, he cut in with a left hook that landed on the side of Shoo Lee's face.

Samuel Jones hovered around the fighters, watching for rule infractions. Shoo Lee's head rocked back at the impact of Kennedy's left fist, which slipped on the Vaseline but left a reddening welt behind. Shoo Lee let a whoosh of air from his lungs and shouted, 'Yah, yah, yah,' punctuating each shout with solid blows to Kennedy's midriff, left and right and left again.

The crowd rumbled to see the big Irishman bend over, as Shoo Lee pounded his guts. Then Kennedy went to his knees.

'Halt,' Samuel Jones shouted. 'Round over. One minute of rest at your own corners.' He pointed Kennedy to his beer barrel. Shoo Lee went back to his as well.

'He can take punishment,' Shawn

Brodie said to Shoo Lee. 'Irishmen can be tough.'

Shoo Lee grunted.

Samuel Jones came to look at Shoo Lee's face. It was slightly red and swollen. No reason to call off the fight. He crossed to Kennedy's corner. The marks of Shoo Lee's fists were red splotches on Kennedy's thick white belly. The fighter took deep breaths, trying to relax in his allotted one minute of rest.

'Stand,' Jones said. His voice carried to the furthest of the spectators. The crowd murmured. They didn't seem as sure of Kennedy's victory as before. Kennedy and Shoo Lee stood.

'Advance to the center,' Jones said. He beckoned to the fighters. They walked to within a long stride of each other. 'Resume the fight,' Jones shouted, and stepped back out of the way.

'Aarrrgh.' Kennedy moved toward Shoo Lee, his arms moving like pistons in front of his body. He bulled ahead as if he knew he could overpower the smaller Chinaman. But when he closed, Shoo Lee's forearms worked like wooden bats, knocking Kennedy's punches aside. Shoo Lee backed slowly away as Kennedy pushed forward, but none of the Irishman's punches landed. The crowd growled. The fight wasn't going to their liking. Sweat formed on Kennedy's face and rolled down his hairy white chest. He began to struggle to get enough air to fuel his piston-like punches. He slowed. The power of his punches waned.

Shoo Lee's eyes narrowed. He kept Kennedy moving in a circle, stepping or jumping lightly back and around as he parried the heavy Irishman's blows. Shoo Lee leaped forward and up into the air, 'Kyaaah'. He screeched a cry that hardened his stomach muscles and added to the momentum of his slicing blow. The horn-hard edge of his right hand bludgeoned the side of Kennedy's neck, stunning the nerves and cutting off blood going to the Irishman's head for an instant. Kennedy fell to one knee, dazed.

'Halt!' Samuel Jones shouted. 'Round over.' He stepped between the fighters.

'Butch! Hey, Butch. We got all our money riding on you, asshole.' The workman hollering at Kennedy, who sat slumped on his beer keg, frothed at the mouth, his face red with booze and anger. 'You hear me, champ? You lose this fight and your ass is mud. Pure mud, I say.'

'Pud's got that right,' shouted another. 'Come on, champ. Chop the Chink up in little pieces.'

The crowd took up the chant. 'Chop the Chink. Chop the Chink. Chop the Chink.'

The denizens of Chinkburg, who now stood eight to ten deep back of Shoo Lee's corner, said nothing. They looked at the chanters, but their eyes were flat. Their quiet confidence showed clearly. Shawn Brodie leaned close to Shoo Lee to say something into his ear. Shoo Lee nodded.

Samuel Jones checked his watch. 'One-minute rest period is over. Stand and advance to the center.'

Shoo Lee stood immediately and strode to a position near the center of the ring. He said nothing, nor did he look at anything other than his opponent, the big Irishman, Butch Kennedy.

'Kennedy,' Jones said. 'Continue the bout, or throw the towel in.'

Kennedy stood. He took a deep breath. The rage of confidence no longer showed on his face. Instead, perhaps he wondered if he'd come out of the bout alive. He shuffled toward the center of the ring where Shoo Lee waited with his hands dangling at his sides and his feet spread slightly more than shoulder-width apart. Kennedy waggled his head, seeming to test his neck where Shoo Lee's hand had struck. He shrugged his shoulders and lifted his fists to a fighting stance, but he didn't carry the fight to Shoo Lee as before. Instead, he stopped slightly more than an arm length away. He lunged at Shoo Lee, stabbing out with a right jab.

Shoo Lee moved only enough for Kennedy's jab to miss.

Kennedy tried a left hook.

Again, Shoo Lee was not there, and Kennedy's fist smashed only air.

A shout came from the crowd. 'Stand still like a man, asshole Chink.'

Shoo Lee smiled and made a little bow. He dodged from Kennedy's path, and the Irishman's fists cut empty air. The smile stayed on Shoo Lee's face. The crowd's roar took on a very nasty edge.

11

'Take 'im, Butch. He cain't get away. We'll catch the bugger if he runs.'

'That we will, Kennedy.'

Kennedy didn't look at the men who shouted at him, he stared only at the stocky figure of Shoo Lee, a man he was fighting just because the stupid Chinaman wouldn't accept the usual half-pay for Chinks. He shifted his glare to Samuel Jones. Damn gambler. This here fight was his idea in the first place. Kennedy shook his head. He had to concentrate on Shoo Lee, but couldn't seem to get his mind to work right. He clenched and unclenched his fists, then pounded his right fist into the palm of his left hand. He got his dukes up, as they say, and went after the Chinaman.

Right cross. Hit only air. Left jab, slipped off the slick Vaseline on Shoo Lee's face and neck. Right straight, glancing blow. Left hook, missed. Wham. Wham. Wham. Three punches from rock-hard fists with knuckles thickened in mare's piss smashed into Kennedy's sternum. The bones cracked and pain flashed through Kennedy's brain. He doubled over and slowly went to his knees. Only his Irish manhood kept him from screaming in pain.

'Time.' Samuel Jones's shout registered dimly in Kennedy's ears. 'Round over!'

Now the crowd was silent. Every eye was on Butch Kennedy. He struggled to his feet, shaking his head like he couldn't believe what was happening.

'To your corner,' Jones said. He turned Kennedy around and gave him a little shove toward the beer keg that served as the corner seat. The Irishman stumbled to the keg and sat.

'You all right, Butch?' Bobby McGilly, Kennedy's second, said. 'Only a couple of punches to the gut, eh? Stuff you take every day of the year, right?'

Kennedy didn't dare try to talk. He'd

groan if he opened his mouth to talk. He breathed as shallowly as he could. Deep breaths brought shooting pains to his breastbone.

'Whiskey,' McGilly said, pushing a bottle into Kennedy's hand.

'No drinking during the bout,' Jones called, shaking his head. He strode toward Kennedy's corner. 'Are you calling it quits, Kennedy? Hum?'

Kennedy straightened his back. 'Not likely,' he said in a quiet voice. 'Not very goldurn likely.' He looked across the ring at Shoo Lee, who sat motionless on his keg, legs crossed at the ankles, hands on his thighs with his fingers held in funny positions. *Who in hell is that man?* He didn't like the shit-eating smile on that Chink's face. Anger began to boil again, and the adrenalin it sent surging through his body held the pain in his chest to a dull ache.

'Time,' Samuel Jones hollered. 'Fighters up and at it.'

Kennedy got to his feet, squinting at

the pain that lanced through his chest from his cracked breastbone. He'd have to make sure the Chink couldn't get to that sore spot. He doubled his fists and put his forearms out in front to ward off any punches from head on. He shuffled toward the center of the ring.

He watched Shoo Lee through hooded eyes, trying to detect any kind of signal that would mean the Chinaman was going to throw a punch. There was none. The Chink walked toward Kennedy casually, taking no fighting stance at all. Kennedy kept his fists under his chin and his forearms closed to protect his chest. He shuffled. It seemed that Shoo Lee speeded up, came faster, but didn't seem to be aiming at Kennedy's injured chest as any smart fighter would do. And he still had that shit-eating half-smile on his Chinky face.

Shoo Lee moved to his right, circling around Kennedy, who pivoted to keep his guard toward the Oriental.

'Bust his butt, Butch,' hollered an

onlooker. 'Beat his ass dead.'

Kennedy wished he could, but his chest was starting to hurt again as the adrenalin wore off. He took shallow breaths through his nose. It didn't help. He turned to keep his guard where the Chinaman was likely to hit. *God, it hurts*.

Then he lost sight of Shoo Lee. Where'd he go? Kennedy turned his head left and right, trying to spot the Chinaman. Shoo Lee leaped out in front of Kennedy, who struggled to get into the proper defensive stance again. The Chinaman whirled, letting his right arm follow his body around, building centrifugal force. Kennedy put his arms up to bar a strike from the front, but Shoo Lee's arm came around from the side and his hard middle knuckle smashed deep into Kennedy's unprotected temple. The Irishman dropped to his knees like he'd been shot, then crumpled over on to his side.

'Damn Chinaman killed Butch! Smashed him dead. I seen it.'

'Quiet!' Samuel Jones roared. He strode to Kennedy's side and felt his neck. 'Knocked out cold. No one in this ring is dead. But Shoo Lee has won this bout by a knockout.'

Shoo Lee bowed to Jones. 'Thank you,' he said. 'You are a fair man.'

Jones gave Shoo Lee a hard look. 'No one cheats at my table, Chinaman, no one. You beat Kennedy fair and square. Some will be happy you did. Others will be very angry.'

Almost in answer to Jones's announcement of Shoo Lee's win, the crowd of Diablo denizens who had bet on Kennedy to win started getting rowdy. Shouts of 'Kill the Chink'. 'Cut that slant-eye down'. 'Put 'im out like he put Butch out, only dead out'.

Shawn Brodie stepped to Shoo Lee's side and said something to him. Shoo Lee nodded and slipped into the crowd of people from Chinkburg.

'Where'd the Chink go?' 'Get his ass, he owes us, by the heavens, he does.' Globs of men pushed and shoved, trying their best to get to a position where they could get at Shoo Lee.

A shotgun went off and the crowd stopped dead still. As one, heads turned toward Poker Flat.

'The Chinaman won the fight fair and square,' Guy Rankin hollered. 'Anyone tries to cross them tracks to Chinkburg and us Lazy EP riders'll have us a turkey-shoot.' Rankin broke open the double-barreled Greener 10-gauge in his hands, plucked the spent shells from the breech, and pushed in two new ones. He snapped the shotgun closed with a flick of his wrist and settled the cannon-like muzzles on the crowd. On either side of Rankin two Lazy EP men stood with Winchesters cocked and ready. No one in the crowd wanted to test the shooting ability of five determined men.

'Thanks, Rankin,' Shawn said as he climbed the steps to the porch of Poker Flat. 'Maybe this way people who bet on Shoo Lee can get paid. I'll push on in and collect for me and the boss.'

'Keno Harry put ours aside,' Rankin said. 'Don't you worry.'

Shawn entered Poker Flat casually, with every sense alert. People knew he stood in Shoo Lee's corner, and many were upset at his win.

Keno Harry paid out winnings from behind the mahogany bar, carefully checking his tally book and confirming the claimed payout before actually dealing out the cash.

Shawn waited patiently for his turn. 'Anyone come in from Chinkburg,' he asked when he reached the bar.

Keno Harry shook his head.

'You make sure to hold their winnings, Harry. Wouldn't like to hear of anyone falling short.'

'Let me worry about that.'

'Shoo Lee tells me someone's short, I'll come visiting,' Shawn said. 'No threat, but I'll want to know the whys and wherefores.'

Keno Harry nodded. 'I'm good for it,' he said.

'I'll take my payout,' Shawn said, 'and I'll head back to Winslow with the boss's payout as soon as the train leaves, so you might as well give me his.'

Again, Keno Harry nodded. 'Lot o' cash to carry around,' he said, almost whispering. ''Specially here in this town. Let me do this.' He raised his voice. 'You going to Winslow, ain'cha? I'll give you a bank draft on Wells Fargo, then. In your name, won't be no good to no one else.' Harry's voice easily carried to every ear in the room. 'Won't be too many people wanting to bust you for your gold if all you've got is worthless paper.'

Shawn had to laugh. 'Damned if you ain't got it right. Who'd shoot me down for a worthless piece of paper?'

'Hang on.' Keno Harry left his spot behind the bar and hustled into the back room. Moments later he came back waving a bank draft. 'Here ya go, Brodie.' He didn't say the amount. 'You take your share in Winslow and give the rest to Peel.'

'Will do,' Shawn said. He accepted the draft and put it away without even looking at it. 'Thank you, Harry. You run a good shop.'

'You think so, kid? Have a try at Samuel Jones when you get back in town. He'll take you for every cent you've got.'

Shawn shook his head and chuckled. 'Me and Sam Jones got a deal going. He don't cheat on me and I don't cheat on him. No one loses, everyone wins.' He held his hand above his head, waggled his fingers, and headed for the door. 'See ya when I get back, Harry,' he said.

Outside, Rankin and the Lazy EP boys still stood on the porch, but the crowd had broken up. He heard Shawn approach and gave him a sidelong look. 'Get paid?' he asked.

'Got a piece of paper.'

'What the hell for?'

'No good to anyone else. Take it to Wells Fargo, they give me cash money.'

Shawn leaned on the porch railing. 'Give me the Greener. I'll watch things while you get paid off. Then the boys can take turns.'

Rankin handed Shawn the shotgun, then dug a handful of 10-gauge shells out of his pocket. 'Just in case,' he said, and gave them to Shawn. 'Be back in a jiffy.' He plunged through the door into Poker Flat.

Grumbling and looking sideways at the Lazy EP riders, the crowd broke up into groups of three or four men. The doves who'd come out to watch Butch pound the Chink to smithereens had long gone back to their positions by the bars of Diablo. Many men disappeared through the doors of Hell Street drinkeries, but some lingered, out of cash, perhaps, because of Shoo Lee's win. The Lazy EP riders kept their watchful stance.

One by one the Lazy EP cowboys collected their winnings from Keno Harry.

'Damn near made me a stake,'

Rankin said. 'Thanks to you, Shawn. Come on back in. Buy you a drink.'

Shawn held up a hand. 'Thanks, boss, but I gotta take the train back to Winslow and I'd better see Shoo Lee before it leaves.' He handed the Greener back to the Lazy EP *segundo*. 'You boys better stay bunched up. Might be a good idea to beeline for the ranch.'

Rankin grinned. 'And who are you to be telling me what to do, kid?'

Shawn shrugged, a grin on his face as well. 'Free country,' he said. 'Man can speak his mind, I hear.'

'Common mistake, that.'

'I reckon.'

'You take care over in Chinkburg. Don't want to hear of you getting kilt.'

'Will do, boss.' Shawn went down the steps to Hell Street. He scanned left and right. Off to the right, Hell Street ended at the edge of Canyon Diablo, less than 200 yards away. To Shawn's left, the street ran parallel with the Atlantic & Pacific tracks. The raw

clapboard and plank-and-batten buildings along Hell Street were already
gray, though most were hardly two
years old. The A&P station, built of
stone and painted yellow, seemed to
glow in the sun, and the steel rails
winked shiny and silver between the
buildings. Little moved.

Hell Street was wide, as a main street
should be, with room enough for a
freight wagon pulled by half a dozen
mules to turn around.

Lazy EP riders stood on the porch of
Poker Flats, guns ready, watching
Shawn cross Hell Street. He glanced
over his shoulder at them just before
crossing the tracks. Rankin put a finger
to the brim of his Stetson and Shawn
waved back. Then he turned his
attention to Chinkburg.

No streets. Nothing more than
narrow pathways for people who
walked. The abodes of Chinkburg were
different from those on the north side
of the tracks. Some were adobe. Some
were stone, chinked with mud. Some

were wikiup-like huts of brush, with and without canvas covers.

Shawn strode south toward a knot of people. In Mexico, a man would think a fiesta'd started up, but the Chinkburg crowd was Oriental, mostly. Still, they hopped around and hollered like they'd just struck the mother lode, which perhaps they had.

Closer, Shawn saw Shoo Lee, stoic as ever, but his eyes sparkled. He didn't mind being the most popular man in Chinkburg, obviously. Shawn pushed his way through the crowd.

'Shawn Brodie.' Shoo Lee shoved out a hard hand.

'Shoo Lee.' Shawn took the hand. The hard grip, his and Shoo Lee's, spoke of friendship carved from months and years in the same cell at Yuma's Hell Hole.

'Come,' Shoo Lee said. He held both hands above his head and said something in Chink talk. The crowd opened and he beckoned for Shawn to follow.

The crowd came, too, but was not as

boisterous as before. Shoo Lee led the way to Yu Wanglim's opium den. 'We can talk in here,' he said.

Inside, the thick air bore the sweetish smell of opium smoke. Already men lay on the board pallets, an opium pipe handy.

Shoo Lee spoke to Yu, who led them between the three-tier pallets into a small room behind the smoking room. He took one chair at a small round table and beckoned Shawn to another. Yu disappeared back into the smoky den. Moments later a young Chinese girl in a silk-looking dress brought two porcelain cups of fragrant tea.

Shoo Lee said nothing until the girl left.

Shawn sipped at the tea. 'Tastes like flowers smell,' he said.

'Jasmine,' Shoo Lee said. 'Thank you for being my second, Shawn Brodie.'

'You all in Chinkburg're gonna have to lie low for a while,' Shawn said.

'We always do. That's how Chinee live in whiteman land.'

'I reckon. But after this fight, the Irishmen'll beat on you all every chance they get.'

'We may move out,' Shoo Lee said.

'Move out?'

'A&P wants me to ramrod the track-laying on to Flagstaff,' Shoo Lee said.

'No shit. Why's that?'

Shards of conversation in language Shawn didn't understand came from the opium room. Shoo Lee leaned across the table. 'I don't promise what I can't do. I don't cheat with the railroad's money. I don't take away money from the people who do the work. I don't.'

'So A&P's come to you, then. How'd they know you can deliver the goods?'

'I cleared the railroad track at ten-mile cut in two days.'

'Why?'

'Robbers made a landslide there. I helped, me and lots of Chinamen and Mexes and blackmen, we cleared the tracks. Wilkinson wants good job done laying track on the other side of Canyon Diablo.'

Shawn tipped his short-brimmed Stetson back on his head. 'Irishmen won't be happy.'

'I'm a sneaky Oriental, you see.' Shoo Lee's smile was more like a tight line across his face.

'Right.' Shawn sipped at the flower-flavored tea. 'Right,' he said again.

Shoo Lee said nothing.

'And how are you going to collect from Keno Harry?'

'You, my friend. You.'

'I gotta go to Winslow.'

'No rush.' Shoo Lee sat motionless, his dark eyes never leaving Shawn's face.

After some moments Shawn nodded. 'When I get back, then.'

'We depend on you, Shawn Brodie. Other whitemen would kill us for the money we won.'

'They may kill you for the A&P contract, too. And make sure you get a contract. Wilkinson seems like a straight man. I reckon he'll get you a written promise.'

'I will insist.'

Someone rapped on the door. 'Yes,' Shoo Lee said.

The little Chinese woman entered. '*Dim sum?*' she asked.

'Deem song?' Shawn said, raising his eyebrows at Shoo Lee.

'What do you say?' Shoo Lee said. 'Very small pieces of food. Many different kinds. Sometimes have when drinking tea.'

'Good?'

'Very.'

'Please bring some deem song, then.'

The young woman giggled. '*Dim sum*, master,' she said.

'That's what I said. Deem some.'

She scurried away and returned as if she'd left the tray of goodies just outside the door. She placed it in the center of the table. '*Dim sum*,' she said.

The large wooden platter held mounds of deep-fried pork squares in thick sauce, little puffy white dumpling-like rolls, other dumplings with thin white skins that showed the meat and vegetables inside, steamed leaves wrapped around something, and little dried fish in sticky sauce, among other things. The platter had a pair of chopsticks for Shoo Lee and a fork for Shawn.

'Very good,' Shoo Lee said. He picked up one of the pork cubes with the chopsticks, popped it into his mouth, chewed, sighed, and swallowed. He sipped some jasmine tea. 'Excellent.'

Just as Shawn forked some pork, Yu Wanglim crashed into the room.

'Whitemen,' he shouted. 'Whitemen coming into our town. Got guns!'

12

Shawn Brodie and Shoo Lee leaped to their feet, the plate of *dim sum* forgotten.

'Guns?' Shawn asked.

'Yes. Yes!' Yu Wanglim cried.

'Not here,' Shoo Lee said, understanding at once what Shawn meant. '*Katana* and *sankakuyari* at my house.'

'Give me your *shuriken*,' Shawn said. 'You run for home, bring me a blade.'

'*Hai*,' Shoo Lee said automatically, even though Shawn was younger and Shoo Lee was his teacher. In this fight, Shawn knew the enemy better. Shoo Lee handed over six throwing-stars, slipped away from the opium den, and disappeared.

Shawn put the throwing-stars in his pants pocket, palmed one of his own from its hiding-place in his clothing and left Yu Wanglim's place at an easy jog. A hundred yards or so away, men lay waste to Chinkburg. Some used sledge-hammers. Some used pickaxes. Some used crowbars. All were intent on tearing down adobe and sandstone huts. A slender woman in what looked like black silk pajamas ran from the angry, cursing mob. She carried an infant, but she ran swift and nimble. One of the mob knelt and steadied his six-gun with two hands. He shot. Missed. Shot again. Missed again. Then the woman ducked behind a stone hut.

Shawn strode directly toward the mob. He took no shelter. He didn't feint or dodge. He just walked, straight and proud.

'Don't you pick on women and children,' he roared. 'Here's a man. See what you can do to him.' He struck his own chest with his left fist.

The mob seemed to be no more than twenty-five or thirty men. Not all had guns, but all seemed intent on tearing Chinkburg down.

The man with the pistol turned his

attention to Shawn. He squinted over the gunsights. Flame and smoke spouted from the pistol, but the bullet struck the ground several feet ahead of Shawn, and whined away over Canyon Diablo.

As his right foot came down and his body's axis shifted to that leg, Shawn used an underhand flick of his wrist to send the *shuriken* throwing-star whirling toward the gunman.

Just before the throwing-star struck, it turned in flight from horizontal to vertical and plunged into the juncture of the gunman's shoulder and neck. He screeched, grabbing at the star, but the sharp tines pricked his fingers. He forgot about trying to shoot the fleeing flock of Chinkburg people. He used both hands, trying to extract the star. Blood leaked from around the sharp tine embedded in his neck. He couldn't pull the star out. In seconds, his hands bled, too. Then Shawn cut his throat with the razor-sharp *tanto* knife he carried in a sheath at the small of his back.

Guns still roared. Sledgehammers still pounded adobes to bits. Crowbars still pried open doors and windows. Weaponless Chinese fled, their pigtails flopping as they ran.

Whites still came across the tracks from Hell Street, but no large gangs gathered. In twos and threes they chased after Chinese, who scampered like rabbits among the huts.

Shawn scooped up the pistol the bleeding man had fired at him and found it was a Smith & Wesson .45 with only one bullet in the cylinder. He shoved the gun behind his waistband and palmed another *shuriken* throwing-star. An instant later, he loosed the star at a big man who lumbered after one of the few Chinese women in Chinkburg.

The beefy man howled as the star took him in the left kidney, burrowing two inches into the muscle along his back. He stumbled to his knees, struggling to reach the *shuriken*.

Shawn stepped to the man's side. 'I

am here,' he said. 'See if you can chase me down and destroy me out of hand.' He held his *tanto* knife low in his right hand, cutting edge out.

'Sumbitch,' the man growled. 'Why'dja stick me? Chinee bitch ain't worth hot shit.'

Shawn sheathed his knife. 'To show you that all men and women are human, I will beat you. Perhaps until you die.' He smashed the man between the eyes from straight ahead, his legs anchored to the ground, his right arm locked at the elbow at the end of the blow, and the two iron-hard knuckles of his hand putting a dent into the man's skull.

As the man crumpled like a poleaxed pig Shawn scanned Chinkburg. Dust rose from running, scrambling, chasing feet. More whites poured across the tracks. Half a hundred men now joined in the destruction of the shanty-town.

'Shawn Brodie!' Shoo Lee's shout cut through the bedlam.

Shawn turned and Shoo Lee tossed

him a six-foot staff. He kept another for himself.

'There,' Shoo Lee said. He pointed at a group of thick-bodied men who'd surrounded three terrified Chinamen.

Shawn plucked the wooden cover from the end of the staff, baring an eight-inch blade. In cross-section the blade was triangular and all three edges were sharp as any well-honed Bowie.

'We go.' Shoo Lee marched toward the group of men, who looked like day workers, men who would ordinarily be waiting in the open space across Hell Street for a job offer. Now they found that kicking cowering Orientals with their thick leather brogans made great entertainment.

Shoo Lee waded into the circle of ruffians, his staff whirling and stabbing. He'd not bared the blade, but used the staff as if he were in Sherwood Forest. Men howled as the three-inch staff smashed into heads, struck shins and elbows, cracked against hands and noses. Shawn followed in Shoo Lee's wake, protecting his back and thumping anyone who thought they could take him from behind.

In moments, they straddled the cowering Chinamen. Shoo Lee said something in Chinese. The Chinamen gathered behind him and crouched between him and Shawn.

'You may not kick my friends,' Shoo Lee said. He didn't shout, but his words were perfectly clear. 'If you leave now, you may have your lives. If you keep trying to destroy our homes, I will kill you. My friend Shawn Brodie will kill you.'

More ruffians gathered, wanting to see what the ruckus was about.

'He's just a slant-eye.'

'He beat the shit outta Butch Kennedy.'

'Ain't no heathen with a stick gonna tell me what to do. I say we rush 'em.'

Shoo Lee pointed the end of his staff at the speaker. 'How many? Ten? Fifteen? You will never have enough to harm me.'

'Gun,' Shawn said.

Shoo Lee's staff flashed out, catching the gunman's wrist as he brought the weapon into line. The bone cracked. The gun clattered to the rocky ground. The man screeched, but Shoo Lee's attention flicked from face to face. The cluster of ruffians was now sober and quiet.

'Go,' said Shoo Lee. 'I do not wish to kill any of you.'

The dust settled in that one small patch of Chinkburg.

Shawn stood with his back to Shoo Lee, his blade bared. 'Better listen to Shoo Lee,' he said. 'No need for any more dead men.'

'Shit. You cain't git us all.'

'Do ya want to find out?' Shawn shifted so that the wicked point of his shaft lined up with the speaker, who took an involuntary step back, away from the gleaming blade. He shook his head.

'Leave. All of you leave,' Shawn said. 'Leave and stay alive.'

A tall Irishman spoke from behind the circle of ruffians. 'Damn it to hell. The Chinks've been squirreling away gold that should rightly b'long to us, and that's sure. We aim for a fair share, that we do.'

Shawn smoothly pulled the Smith & Wesson from his waistband and leveled it at the speaker.

'And what makes you think you've got the right to rob Chinese men, even if they do have savings, which they don't?'

'Sons of Eire said so. Said the heathens have gold. They ain't nothing but god-forsaken heathens, after all, they ain't. Not God's sons, as we from the Emerald Isle are.'

'Bullshit. And you know it.' Shawn felt hot blood rise to his face. 'You motherless micks left your god-forsaken island for a better life here. These men,' Shawn gestured at the cowering Chinese, 'these men left mothers and fathers, wives and children, all back in their homeland, and they send every

217

spare penny back to their families so they won't starve. How 'bout you, mick? You sending anything back to Ireland?'

The man fell silent. Then he scuffed at the rocky path with one of his oversized brogans. He didn't look at Shawn.

'Come on, boyos. Let's get outta here.'

The big Irishman made his way back to the tracks, then turned to survey Chinkburg with baleful eyes. He shook a fist in Shawn's direction, crossed the tracks, and disappeared on Hell Street.

'We should get all the Chinamen together,' Shoo Lee said. 'Easier to defend.'

'Easier said than done.'

Shoo Lee shrugged. He said something to the cowering Chinese. They didn't respond. 'You. Chinee,' he said. 'You get for Yu Wanglim house. Pronto, quick, quick.'

The Chinese men ran down the well-worn path toward the opium house. Shoo Lee and Shawn Brodie began moving from hut to hut, poking and jabbing with their staffs, making it painful for whitemen to be looting in Chinkburg. On the west side, near the lip of Canyon Diablo, a big man with a smith's broad shoulders and bulging biceps used a sledgehammer to reduce an adobe hut to clods. He handled the twelve-pound sledge like it was a toy, smashing its ponderous head against the remaining wall.

'Enough, Paddy,' Shawn said. 'Time to get back across the tracks.'

The big man stopped, the hammer over his shoulder ready for the next swing. 'I ain't no Paddy,' he said.

'Then you shouldn't be mobbing up with Irishmen.'

'And what makes you think you can tell me what to do and what not to do?'

'I'm asking you,' Shawn said. 'No one deserves to have a mob after them. Not even Chinese. Do me a favor. Go back across the tracks.'

'Favor? Who are you to ask a favor?'

'Shawn Brodie. Shoo Lee, the man who beat Butch Kennedy to a standstill, was my cellmate at Yuma.'

'Yuma!'

'Yeah. The Hell Hole. Would you do me a favor?'

'Shawn Brodie, is it? I'll be Ridley. No one calls me other than Ridley, though my ma and pa tagged me with George Henry. George Henry Ridley.'

'You're a man, George Henry Ridley. Obliged. I'll even ask one more favor of ya.'

Ridley raised an eyebrow.

'Help me get the micks and those what think there may be loot in Chinkburg back across the tracks. Tell them there's free drinks at Keno Harry's Poker Flat. Tell Sam Jones to foot the bill, a drink each, and I'll make it up to him.'

Ridley hefted his hammer. 'A drink at Poker Flat?'

'The same,' Shawn said.

'I'll do it,' Ridley said. He shouldered

the hammer and strode away, headed for another hammer-wielder. They spoke for a moment, then moved off together.

'What did you do?' Shoo Lee's question came from behind Shawn.

'They're finding precious little loot in Chinkburg,' Shawn said. 'I reckon the work of tearing down people's houses is starting to get tiresome.' He waved at Ridley. 'He's inviting people to have a drink, on me.'

Ridley gathered a dozen sweating men, who threaded their way through Chinkburg toward the A&P tracks. Others, seeing the crowd, came to join. Ridley grinned as the men passed Shawn and Shoo Lee.

'Free drink,' he said. 'Shawn Brodie, gentleman that he is, is buying.'

'Good man, George Henry Ridley. I'll be along directly. But you tell Sam Jones and Keno Harry, and they'll set those drinks up. Trust me.'

Ridley turned and made a megaphone with his hands. 'Yeee haw,' he shouted. 'Drinks on Mr Brodie. Come along.'

Heads came up. Sweaty faces covered with clay dust. Eyes red. Hands empty. All the effort in Chinkburg had brought little, precious little. Thirst took over. Ridley's followers increased from a dozen to two dozen. He waved an arm. 'Come on. Drink's free. Ain't nothing for us here. Come on!'

Horsemen clattered across the track into Chinkburg, Winchesters held like lances on the rider's thighs. They formed a line along the tracks, facing Chinkburg, leaving a space wide enough for Ridley's thirsty men to get back to Hell Street.

'Lazy EP riders,' Shawn said to Shoo Lee.

The fever of the Chinkburg invaders faded. The dust settled. A slight breeze came down the canyon from the south. Cottonball clouds marched in rows across a brassy blue sky. What started off to be a massacre, turned into an embarrassment. A thought ran across

Shawn Brodie's mind. *What will the whitemen do when they find out Shoo Lee is to ramrod the construction of the A&P railroad on the west side of Canyon Diablo?*

Lazy EP riders surrounded the remaining whitemen.

'Heeyah,' Guy Rankin hollered, slapping his leather chaps with a coiled lariat. He looked like he was chousing steers out on the Colorado Plateau.

Other Lazy EP men followed Rankin's lead. Dust-covered whitemen slouched their way through the ruins of Chinkburg adobes, herded by cowboys.

'Free drinks on Mr Brodie,' big George Ridley hollered from the tracks. 'Keno Harry's setting them up in Poker Flat.'

Suddenly the rush was on. Men who'd been chasing Chinese only moments before now clamored to cross the tracks for the promised free liquor.

Shoo Lee stood shoulder to shoulder with Shawn Brodie. 'My thanks to you,

Shawn. As ever, you do what is best to do. For everybody but Shawn Brodie, that is.'

Shawn glanced sideways at the man who had saved his life more than once in Yuma prison. 'I owe you more than I can every repay,' he said. He bowed his head in thought. 'Ain't none of my business, Shoo Lee, but you mind me saying something?'

'You can say anything to me, my friend. You should already understand that.'

'Shoo Lee. I know Mr Wilkinson hired you to keep on laying A&P tracks on the far side of Canyon Diablo.'

'He did.' Shoo Lee sidled around to where he could look directly into Shawn's face. 'Is that a problem?'

'Look what happened today. Just because you won a fight that lost those men some gambling money. What do you think they'll do when they find out Chinese and Mexicans and blacks get all the railroad work?'

Slowly Shoo Lee nodded. 'Maybe

they kill us all,' he said.

'More than likely. No law in this town, and Winslow and Flagstaff're too far away anyhow. The army's in Camp Verde and Whipple Barracks. Not much help, if any.'

'Shawn,' Shoo Lee said, his face set in lines of determination. 'Important. Very important.'

Shawn watched the last of the mob traipse across the tracks. Lazy EP men closed the gap, then reined their horses toward Hell Street. Guy Rankin waved a farewell to Shawn, and the riders disappeared around the corner.

Shawn took a deep breath. 'Shoo Lee, I'm not trying to tell you what to do, but I'm figuring that you'll hold on to more by sharing the jobs. This don't have to be an all-or-nothing proposition, you know.'

Shoo Lee hooked his head towards the railroad crossing. 'They would take everything,' he said.

'Try it.'

'So. How do we share? How can

whitemen be fair? We're yellow. Or brown. Or black. That means kowtow to whites, they think.' Shoo Lee's eyes widened, showing his anger.

'Not kowtow. But not be unreasonable, either,' Shawn said.

The set of Shoo Lee's mouth, the hard look in his eyes and the balanced spread of his legs said he was not convinced.

Shawn hit on an idea. 'Do you know Sam Jones?'

Shoo Lee nodded.

'He's straight. Never cheats. Don't allow slick stuff at his table. Mind if I talk to him? I'll bet he can steer us down the right path.'

Shoo Lee studied Shawn's face, then turned his own face to the sky and closed his eyes. After a long moment of silence, a small smile came to his lips.

'Sam Jones is the reason we won money today,' he said. 'Butch Kennedy had it in his mind to take half of Chinaman's pay. I refused. Sam backed me up. I think maybe he don't see Chinee to be stinking heathen.'

With the marauding whitemen gone, Chinkburg residents returned to their huts and began sorting through the rubble.

Shoo Lee tilted his head toward one of them. 'Chinee take what comes. Fate. Fortune. Good. Bad. All part of life. Today look black, maybe tomorrow look better. Talk to Sam Jones,' he said. 'Maybe tomorrow will be a brighter day.'

13

Shawn cashed the bank drafts at Wells Fargo in Winslow before going to see Ellison Peel at Doc Kinderly's place.

'Welcome back, young man,' the doctor said. 'From the look on your face I'd say your trip to Diablo and back was worth the time and effort.'

'It was. How's the boss?'

'Much of the feeling in his extremities has returned. Another week should see him ready to return to Diablo.'

'That's good to hear. Can I see him?'

'He went for a walk, which is good for him, you know. Walking, that is. He said something about going to see an old friend. A Mr Evans, if I recall correctly.'

Tin Can. 'I know Mr Evans. I'll just meander over to his place, then.'

'As you will, young man. As you will.'

Doctor Kinderly turned his attention back to the pile of papers and magazines on his desk.

★ ★ ★

The same strongarms were out front of Tin Can's house. They didn't look pleased to see Shawn, but they didn't try to stop him. Inside, the house was dark. Little of the late afternoon sunshine came in. Tin Can had no sight problems, but Shawn knew he liked to stay out of sight. He rapped on the door to the room where Tin Can took care of business.

The bodyguard called Steve opened the door a crack.

'Shawn Brodie to see Tin Can and Ellison Peel.'

Tin Can's voice came from deep inside the room. 'Let him in.'

Steve stepped back and Shawn entered.

'Well, well. Young Shawn Brodie. Ex-convict from Yuma prison.'

'Tin Can. Are you coming down hard on my boss?'

'Ellison Peel? Yeah. I heard he was your boss.' Tin Can laughed. 'So where does that put me?'

'I ride for his brand,' Shawn said. 'Boss, can I join the conversation?'

'Sit down, Shawn,' Peel said.

'What do you have to contribute?' Tin Can's voice had a hard edge under its jovial veneer.

'Boss,' Shawn said, 'me and Tin Can Evans lived at Yuma prison. He tried to cheat me. He lied to me, and he set me up to take a fall. We got along good.'

'Does that mean you're in cahoots with this shyster?' Peel's voice was as cold as his face.

'I do the odd job for him,' Shawn said. 'He told me, boss, that you owed him three thousand dollars and some interest. That right?'

Peel's discomfort showed. 'What business is that of yours?'

Shawn pulled his shirt tail out and unbuckled the money belt that held

Peel's winnings. 'I reckon you could say I brung you a windfall, boss. Shoo Lee won the fight, like I said he would. The odds was just over seven to one. So your bet brought you ten thousand eight hundred dollars.'

'Ten thousand . . . eight hundred . . . dollars?'

'If I could make a suggestion, boss, you could pay off your debt to Tin Can and still have a good chunk of cash for the improvements you were wanting to make at Lazy EP.' Shawn paused. 'What say?' he asked.

'Ten thousand eight hundred dollars,' Peel said. 'Ten thousand eight hundred dollars.'

'What about it, boss? Shouldn't we pay Tin Can what's owed him?'

Peel jerked like he was coming out of a dream. 'Huh? Tin Can? Oh. Yeah.'

'How much do we owe you, Tin Can?' Shawn opened one of the money-belt pockets so that greenbacks showed.

Tin Can licked his lips, his eyes

skewered to the sight of folding money. 'Peel borrowed three thousand a little over a year ago. Payback in six months, he said, but it's been more'n a year. The deal was that he pay me the three thousand, plus three hundred.'

'I paid three hundred so's you'd let me hang on to the three thousand for another six months,' Peel said.

'Six months's gone,' Tin Can said, 'gone purt nigh a whole month.'

'You know I came to pay you another three hundred so you'd give me a little more time.'

'What in hell's name are you grown men dickering about?' Shawn said, exasperation in his voice. 'Boss, you've got more'n enough to pay Tin Can off. Tin Can, you get what's coming to you. Ain't that what you wanted? Huh?'

Neither man answered. Both nodded. Peel counted out $3,000 in folding greenbacks, and $300 more. Then another hundred. 'For the extra week,' he said. He pushed the bills across the table to Tin Can.

Tin Can took his time arranging the bills in piles on the desk in front of him. He counted each bill, examining it before he laid it in its proper place. 'Three thousand four hundred dollars,' he said. 'Principal plus interest.'

'Well,' Shawn said. 'Is my boss's obligation paid?'

'Paid in full,' Tin Can said. 'Full up.'

'Good. We'll leave, then. Come on, boss.'

'All right.' Peel stood. He took up the money belt. 'Let's go.'

Tin Can pulled a Navy Colt from his desk drawer. 'Maybe you'd like to leave that belt on the desk, Peel. Call it extra interest.'

Shawn spoke. 'Tin Can Evans. You don't want to get me on your wrong side. You got no call to take my boss's cash.' As he spoke, he palmed a throwing-star.

Tin Can threw back his head and laughed, but his gun hand never moved and his eyes were cold and icy, glued to the face of Ellison Peel. 'How 'bout it,

233

Peel? Wanna part with the greenbacks and stay alive? Or do you want to die first and part with them anyway?'

'Damn you, Tin Can Evans,' Shawn said. 'I shoulda known better than to bring all that money in here.'

Tin Can chortled. 'You figure how long it takes a no-leg cripple like me to make ten thousand buckaroos? Peel ain't worth nothin', kid. Don't let it bother you.'

'It bothers me, Tin Can. Bothers me all to hell. You put that Colt away now, and me and my boss'll be on our way.'

'You think I can't pull this trigger before you all can make a . . . *Arrrrgh*.'

Shawn flicked his right wrist and the throwing-star sank into Tin Can Evans's right wrist just inside the palm. His fingers sprang open as if pulled by puppet strings. The Colt clattered to the desktop.

As the star flew, Shawn took a quick step to the side of Tin Can's desk. He had his knife out, and laid it along Tin Can's neck.

'Your move, Tin Can,' he said. 'You call for Steve, or any other of your bully boys, 'n' you'll bleed like a stuck pig. I'll see to it.'

He turned to Peel. 'Pick up the cash, boss, and put it back in the belt. I figure Tin Can's trying to rob you means he don't get no interest. Leave him three thousand. Even. And boss, take the Navy, too.'

Ellison Peel packed the greenbacks into the money belt and scooped up the Navy Colt. He automatically lowered the hammer to half-cock, checked the loads, then eared the hammer back again.

'Call in the boys, Tin Can,' Shawn ordered.

Peel stepped off to one side.

'Call 'em.' Shawn emphasized his command with pressure on the knife.

'Steve. Clark. Come in here a minute,' Tin Can called.

A knock came at the door. 'Tin Can?'

Shawn pressed the knife to Tin Can's throat. 'Answer.'

'Yeah, Steve. Come on in.'

In answer to Tin Can's summons the big man called Steve opened the door.

'Come right in,' Shawn said. 'Make sure Clark does the same.'

The two strongarms came in.

'Shed your six-guns,' Shawn said. His knife drew a trickle of blood from the side of Tin Can's neck.

'Asshole,' Steve growled.

'Tin Can ain't dead. He tried to steal my boss's money. Can't let that happen. Drop the hardware.'

'Shit.' Steve and Clark unbuckled their gunbelts and let them fall to the floor.

'Step away. Steve, you to your left, Clark to the right. Away from the guns now.'

The strongarms moved.

'Boss, the guns, please.' Shawn kept his knife at Tin Can's throat.

Peel kept the cocked Navy ready as he picked up the two gun rigs.

'OK,' Shawn said. 'My boss will give me the Navy and we'll sidle on out of

236

here. You listening, Tin Can?'

Tin Can nodded, very carefully.

'Good. You know I've been more than fair with you. You've got what we call a throwing-star in your wrist and three thousand dollars on the desk. You tried to rob one of mine, Tin Can. I can't have that. Understand?'

Again Tin Can nodded.

'Good.' Shawn took his knife away from Tin Can's neck. 'I'll send Doc Kinderly over,' he said. 'No need for your wrist to go septic.'

Peel handed Shawn the Navy Colt. He had a Single Action Army that belonged to one of the strongarms.

'We'll be going now,' Shawn said. 'I'll leave your hardware at the A&P station on our way out. Don't try to follow us.'

The strongarms looked at Tin Can for orders. He gave them a tiny shake of his head.

Shawn took the two gun rigs, hung them over his left arm, and walked two steps behind Ellison Peel for the six blocks back to Doc Kinderly's place. Neither said a word.

'Well, well,' Doc Kinderly said when they entered. 'Patient alive and well. Patient's employee alive and well. That's good. Yes. Very good.'

'Tin Can Evans needs you over to his place, Doc,' Shawn said. 'And if you don't mind, I'll bunk in the boss's room tonight, just in case.'

'Is that right?' Kinderly reached for his black bag of medical necessities. 'I'd best be off to see what the matter is, then.' He bustled out of the house and down the street.

'Tin Can's not a man to let bygones go by,' Shawn said. 'I don't know when or where he'll hit, but he will. Somewhere, sometime, somehow, he will.'

'You sound like you know him well,' Peel said.

Shawn nodded. 'I do. We were in Yuma prison at the same time. He pretty well ran the underbelly of Yuma. He could even manipulate the sergeant of the guard.' Shawn took a deep breath. 'Boss, he hired me to collect the money you owed him.'

'You?'

'Yep. Me.'

'How'd you figure on doing that?'

'I had no idea. Tin Can painted you bad. Said you was trying to take over Diablo. Said lots of things I found out were wrong. But Tin Can tends to exaggerate.'

Peel stood silent, his eyes on Shawn like he expected more explanation.

'I figured it'd be good to get a job with the Lazy EP, even though cowpoke jobs're scarce.'

'You did,' Peel said, his voice hard.

'I did,' Shawn said. 'And I found out you're a good man to work for. As luck would have it, I got you to pay Tin Can what you owed, but I never figured on him trying to take it all.'

'You get anything from the Chinaman's win?'

'Enough.'

Peel nodded.

'Boss?'

Peel looked up. 'What is it?'

'If it's just the same with you, I'd like to stay aboard. The Lazy EP's a good outfit and I'd like to help out.'

Peel said nothing. Then, just when the silence got to be uncomfortable, he spoke.

'Thanks to you, Shawn, the Lazy EP's got cash to get better stock with, cash to sink a new well, and cash to fence off some acreage for alfalfa and corn and wheat. Far as I'm concerned, you're a Lazy EP hand as long as you want to be.'

Shawn grinned. 'That'll be some time, boss. I never really belonged to nothing my whole life. It's good to have a place to call home.'

14

Samuel Jones arrived first. He tipped his hat to Mel Bartlett, who owned Bartlett's Mercantile.

'Anyone here yet?' he asked.

'No one, Samuel,' said Bartlett, 'but the coffee's hot. You go on in.'

Samuel went into the back room of the general store.

Ellison Peel and Shawn Brodie arrived next. Then Butch Kennedy and Harrison Hall, who owned the livery stable. They sipped the good coffee and said nothing.

Ronald Wilkinson came in, followed by Shoo Lee. They took seats.

'What's the goldam Chink doing here?' Butch Kennedy demanded. 'Sam Jones said we was going to talk about jobs, that he did.'

'Shoo Lee told me that you should be allowed to attend, Mr Kennedy,' Wilkinson said.

'He told you? He told *you?* Who's he that he can tell you what to do?'

Shoo Lee stood. He wore California pants with a loose-fitting cotton shirt. His hair was cut short, but not shaved.

'Everyone who comes to Diablo . . . I mean, 'most everyone who comes to Diablo is looking for work. I think so. Now A&P will begin to have work for good men again.'

Every eye turned to Wilkinson. He nodded.

Shoo Lee continued. 'A&P's gonna start laying track on the other side of Canyon Diablo, on to Flagstaff, Williams, down to Prescott, and on to California. That means more work for everyone, if you all will cooperate.'

Kennedy scowled. 'You speak awful good English for a Chink,' he said.

Shoo Lee's lips curved upward in what might have been a smile.

'Mr Kennedy. There are many kinds of Chinamen in Diablo. And I personally, am not of Chinese blood. Mostly, those of us who cannot speak each

242

other's dialect converse in English. I think you will find the Chinese more capable in English than you might imagine.'

'Hmmmph,' Kennedy said.

Shoo Lee took up the discussion again. 'A&P's stockpiled more than five thousand rails in Winslow. It takes nearly four hundred rails to lay a mile of track. That, and twenty-five hundred ties. The ties can be cut and shaped over there, but the rails've got to be hauled from here to the far side.'

'I got hard-pulling mules,' Harrison Hall said. 'An' I can get more if we need 'em. I reckon you'll want the rails hauled downstream to Tolchico Crossing and then up on to the west rim.'

'Are there wagons and loaders?'

'Have ta make wagons. I've got the wheels and axles, so it won't take more than a week, maybe ten days.'

'Mr Kennedy,' Shoo Lee said. 'May I ask you to be foreman of the whiteman work crews?'

'Why me?'

'I fought with you. I used fighting methods you never saw or experienced before. Still, you did not cry foul, you merely pressed your attack. I think Butch Kennedy works hard to keep his word, once it is given.'

Kennedy thrust his chest out and took a deep breath. 'Every man worth his salt does that.'

Shoo Lee showed his faint smile again. 'Not all, Butch Kennedy. Some feel that cheating Chinamen is just part of the run, is that not right?'

Kennedy couldn't hold Shoo Lee's gaze. 'I reckon,' he said in a small voice.

'Will you please ramrod the white-man teams? I think two tracklayer teams of ten men each to start would be the right balance.'

'Balance with what?'

'With two Chinese teams the same size in terms of numbers. The amount paid each team will depend on how much track is laid.'

'Not by the month?'

Shoo Lee shook his head. 'Some people spend much time drinking coffee or spirits. We do not wish to pay for time that way.'

'We?'

'Mr Wilkinson and I,' Shoo Lee said. 'He pays the money, but it is up to me, and to you, Butch Kennedy, to see that A&P gets its money's worth.'

Kennedy shrugged.

Shoo Lee folded his arms and kept a bland eye on Kennedy.

Kennedy shrugged again. 'Everyone looks for an edge, Chink,' he said.

'As I said, Butch Kennedy, I am not Chinese by birth, though many of our physical features look the same. You may call me Shoo Lee, if you like. Either that, or boss.'

'Boss!'

Shoo Lee nodded. 'As far as A&P Railroad is concerned, Mr Wilkinson has turned authority for the project over to me.'

'She-it.'

'A problem?'

'She-it. Taking orders from a goldam Chinaman.'

Samuel Jones spoke. 'Wilkinson asked Shoo Lee to take over building this railway on the far side of Diablo. He wants the whole town to benefit, not just a few Chinamen ... excuse me, Shoo Lee.'

'The whole town?' Kennedy looked incredulous. 'Why? Where I come from, it's every man for himself.'

Samuel gave Kennedy a long look. 'Now, Mr Kennedy, if there's a man who knows that's not true, it's you. Where's the Irishman who's not willing to help another?'

Kennedy sputtered. 'But ... but ... but that's Irishman to Irishman,' he said.

'And how many Irishmen are there in Diablo?'

'A couple a hundred, not counting saloon- and dance-hall owners.'

'If they can do the job, there will be work,' said Shoo Lee.

'What's that mean?'

'Look, Kennedy. I beat you with my fists. I can do it any time, night or day. You'd better believe that. And I can beat you with my brain. That's why it's me here instead of you. No one gets a job because he knows someone or is related to someone or is an old friend of someone. He gets a job because he can get work done, and done on time.'

Kennedy had no retort.

'Do you want to ramrod the whitemen?' Shoo Lee asked. 'If not, there are others, I think.'

'Don't like taking orders from a Chinaman,' Kennedy said. 'No way. Ain't right. Ain't Christian, an' I'm not gonna stand for it. No way.'

This was not the blustering Butch Kennedy everyone knew. This was a man whom anger had turned ice-cold. White showed where the muscles tensed around his mouth.

'Shoo Lee,' he said, 'don't you get all high and mighty, asshole Chink.'

Kennedy jammed his battered hat on

247

his head. 'You'll not find an Irishman in this whole damn town who'll work for a goldam chinky-eyed Chinaman!' He stormed across the room to the door, wrenched it open, and stomped through the mercantile to Hell Street.

'Play hell to get the Irishmen to cooperate,' Samuel Jones said. 'Pure hell.'

Shoo Lee scratched at his jaw. 'Enough Chinamen and Mexes and Blacks, if A&P don't mind. I gave the Irishmen the opportunity to work. It was Butch Kennedy who took their jobs away, not me.'

The men in the back room of Bartlett Mercantile sat at the big walnut table, which had seen better days, and planned the job of laying track to Flagstaff. When they left the sun had long disappeared over the San Francisco Peaks and a pure white moon stood halfway up a purple-black sky.

★　★　★

'Mind if I sit in?'

Samuel Jones looked up from his cards. 'Take a chair,' he said.

Shawn Brodie dragged a chair out from the table, turned it around, and sat so he could rest his folded arms on its back.

'What's this I hear about Butch Kennedy?'

'Dead.'

'Who done it?'

'No way of knowing. People turn up dead in Diablo all too often. Besides, people kinda blamed him for turning the railroad against the Irish.'

'Too bad. Coulda been good for a few more years, I reckon. You?'

Samuel Jones opened his arms to the nearly empty room. 'Few sheep to fleece,' he said. 'It's about time I moved along. May try San Francisco. Or go back to New Orleans. You?'

Shawn shrugged. 'I like cowboying at the Lazy EP. But come winter, I'll get some time off. Ride down to Yuma.'

'What's in Yuma?'

Shawn grinned. 'Beauty,' he said. 'Pure dee la beauty.'

'Sounds like gold. Hadn't heard of any gold in Yuma,' Samuel said.

Shawn blushed. 'She's pure gold all right. And I've been away too long.'

'Ah. A fair maiden.'

Shawn nodded.

'With Kennedy dead, the Irishmen have gone to Shoo Lee. He's put some to work, but it's all on the west bank. Keno Harry's already set up. Got a tent about halfway between here and Flagstaff. Calls it Winona. Who knows why.'

'Lazy EP's doing good. Lotsa people wanting beef. Boss says I got a job as long as I want one.' Shawn stood up. 'I'll be getting back to the spread. Boss sent me over to get some supplies from Mel.'

'Take care, Shawn.'

'Always,' Shawn said. He raised a finger to the brim of his hat, a salute to Samuel Jones, then shoved his way out the door of Poker Flat.

A bullet tore a chunk from the door

frame as Shawn left. He dropped as if shot, palming a slim knife as he fell.

Footfalls vibrated through the ground as Shawn waited, prostrate and motionless. He lay on his side, knees pulled up in a semi-fetal position, as if he'd taken a bullet in the guts.

'Got 'im. Chink-lovin' bum-licker. Got 'im!' The pounding of running feet came through the hardened surface of Hell Street. Shawn tensed inwardly, the sliver of a knife held lightly in the fingers of his right hand, hidden from sight, but ready for use.

The feet came to a stop. 'He ain't moved since I shot 'im. Chink lover. Deserves to be dead. Big Butch's dead. Only deserving that Chink-lover cowboy gets dead, too.'

'You take it easy, Barry,' said another voice. 'That cowpoke's sneaky as a diamondback.'

'Yeah? Watch out.'

Shawn now had three opponents.

'Dead, I tell ya.' A hand took hold of Shawn's shoulder.

Shawn uncoiled like a striking rattler. A glance showed him a target and the slim knife slid through the eye of the man called Barry and into his brain. He dropped, dead before he hit the dust of Hell Street. Now on his feet, Shawn whirled to face the other two men.

'Gentlemen.' Samuel Jones's voice was interrupted by double clicks of shotgun hammers being eared back. The gambler stood in the doorway, the bar Greener in his hands. The men froze.

'Thank you, Samuel,' Shawn said. He wiped the blood from his knife on the downed man Barry's shirt. The other two took a step back as Shawn moved toward them. Samuel Jones held the scattergun with nonchalant ease; its muzzle seemed drawn to the men as if by magnetism.

'Drag him off,' Shawn said, 'before I get tempted to stick you all, too.'

Each man grabbed an arm and dragged dead Barry away.

'Thank you, Samuel,' Shawn repeated.

'Always figured you for a gentleman.'

'Welcome, young man. Never was one to take unfair advantage.'

'I'll be getting back to the Lazy EP then,' Shawn said. 'See ya when I see ya.' He raised a finger to the brim of his hat.

Samuel Jones stood in the doorway of Poker Flat as Shawn Brodie mounted the bay horse he called General, and reined the gelding toward Bartlett's Mercantile.

'Cute kid,' Maisie said. She shoved her little Derringer back into its hiding place.

'He's a man, dear Maisie. Just the kind of man this country needs.' He looked down at Maisie's upturned face. 'I think we've fleeced all the sheep hereabouts,' he said. 'How would you like to go to Prescott? I hear Whiskey Row offers only the best . . . and the worst.'

'Let's go,' she said.

We do hope that you have enjoyed reading this large print book.

Did you know that all of our titles are available for purchase?

We publish a wide range of high quality large print books including:
Romances, Mysteries, Classics
General Fiction
Non Fiction and Westerns

Special interest titles available in large print are:
The Little Oxford Dictionary
Music Book, Song Book
Hymn Book, Service Book

Also available from us courtesy of Oxford University Press:
Young Readers' Dictionary
(large print edition)
Young Readers' Thesaurus
(large print edition)

For further information or a free brochure, please contact us at:
Ulverscroft Large Print Books Ltd.,
The Green, Bradgate Road, Anstey,
Leicester, LE7 7FU, England.
Tel: (00 44) 0116 236 4325
Fax: (00 44) 0116 234 0205

DIG TWO GRAVES

Peter Wilson

When the town's newspaper office is burned to the ground and the owner murdered, suspicion falls on Lane Cutler, the young deputy marshal of Progress. His alibi — that he was being held prisoner by ruffians at the time of the killing — persuades veteran lawman Ben McCabe to go in search of the truth. But the marshal runs into a wall of silence, shored up by blackmail and revenge. And when death strikes again, McCabe must join forces with a stranger before the final showdown . . .